For more than forty years,
Yearling has been the leading name
in classic and award-winning literature
for young readers.

Yearling books feature children's
favorite authors and characters,
providing dynamic stories of adventure,
humor, history, mystery, and fantasy.

Trust Yearling paperbacks to entertain,
inspire, and promote the love of reading
in all children.

OTHER YEARLING BOOKS YOU WILL ENJOY.

J.B.CHEANEY

My Friend the Enemy

A YEARLING BOOK

To Tielman,
for lots of reasons,
but especially
for Japan

Published by Yearling, an imprint of Random House Children's Books
a division of Random House, Inc., New York

Yearling and the jumping horse design are registered trademarks of Random House, Inc.

Visit us on the Web! www.randomhouse.com/kids
Educators and librarians, for a variety of teaching tools,
visit us at www.randomhouse.com/teachers

ISBN: 978-0-440-42102-3

Reprinted by arrangement with Alfred A. Knopf Books for Young Readers

Printed in the United States of America
August 2007
10 9 8 7 6 5 4 3
First Yearling Edition

CONTENTS

DOING OUR PART

I didn't mean to do it. I just got carried away.

First I found the balloon in the bib pocket of my overalls and thought it would be fun to fill it with water from the faucet by the garage. Then I thought about finding something to throw the balloon at, and that's when my sister put the record on. Dance music blared out of our bedroom window, pulling me closer to the house as the Andrews Sisters sang,

Don't sit under the apple tree
With anyone else but me,

Anyone else but me,
Anyone else but me—No! No! No!

Sneaking around the corner of the house between the for-
sythia bushes, I became patrol leader H. N. Anderson. My men
crept behind me so silently I couldn't even hear them until we
all crouched together under the window, hugging our grenades
and listening to high heels click on the wood floor. Nice trick, I
thought—the enemy's using an all-American band as cover for
sabotage. But it won't work. Steady, men . . . steady . . . NOW!

I leapt up and hurled my grenade through the open window. There wasn't any time to aim; all I hoped to hit was the
floor. But the balloon struck the edge of the vanity mirror and
exploded all over ribbons, lipstick, powder boxes, and Estelle. I
stared at her for a second, seeing mainly a mouth as wide as a
bathtub. Mission accomplished—now scram! I dashed toward
the front porch as my sister's scream sounded—low at first but
zooming up like an air-raid siren. Enemy plane! Take cover!

Straight ahead was the old henhouse. Follow me, men! The
natives might give us shelter! I didn't see the attack squad until
they were right on top of us—trapped! I dodged to the left, but
a long arm reached out and yanked me up so fast my feet swung
out from under me. That made me really mad. "Lemme go, you
lousy Jap!"

"Hey, soldier. Hey. I'm on your side. Private J. J. Lanski, U.S.
Marines." As my heart slowed down, I got an eyeful of starchy

khakis and the gleam of an anchor-and-globe pin on a collar. He stuck out his hand. "Shake."

From the porch Estelle hollered, "Jed! Don't let her get away!"

I remembered the mission and made a bolt for the woods, but Jed caught me around the middle and tucked me under his arm like a bag of flour. Then he started for the house. "Looks like you've seen some action, soldier. You'll have to tell me about it at the picnic."

But Estelle was already telling him, fast and loud. "You'll never guess what she did! I was standing in front of the mirror when she hauls off and throws a water balloon through the window. Now look at me—she's ruined my dress, my hair—"

Which was baloney. The ruffle on one sleeve hung limp, but a little water couldn't wash the curl out of her hair or the sparkle from her eyes. "Oh, dry up," I muttered once my feet were on the ground.

"If only I *could*—"

"I think you look fine," Jed offered. "Better than fine."

They were starting to go all moony-eyed when Mom stalked out of the kitchen, wiping her hands on her apron. "What's going on?"

Estelle started off making it sound like she was Poland and I was Hitler, but Mom cut it short. "All right, all right. For heaven's sake, Hazel, you're almost twelve. Aren't you a little old for silly practical jokes?"

Questions like this don't usually expect an answer.

"Don't let her ride to the picnic with us," Estelle said quickly. "Put her to work washing dishes."

"If I need suggestions, I'll ask for them, dear."

"But *Mother*. It's our last chance to be together before Jed—"

"Um . . . we won't exactly be alone, doll." Jed's fingers twitched on my shoulder, but I wasn't the doll he meant. "My mom decided to come."

We all stared at the Lanskis' Ford. Jed's mother got out of her house so seldom, it was as if a big mushroom had suddenly sprung up in the backseat—a mushroom that colored its lips victory red, fanned itself with a magazine, and waved at us with a pale puffy hand. Estelle sighed all the way down to her shoes but managed not to say anything.

Mom smoothed her apron over her skirt. "Hazel, I expect you'd better stay here and help me clean up the kitchen. You can ride to the picnic later with Aunt Ruth and me. Estelle, you go on and have a good time, but I want you home by dark. You hear, Jed?"

Jed nodded solemnly. Estelle, all smiles again, disappeared into the house—"I'll be right back!" Mom marched out to have a few neighborly words with Mrs. Lanski. I stayed right where I was, stiff as a board.

Jed turned me toward him, but I didn't even unfold my arms. "No hard feelings, okay?"

When I didn't answer, he leaned closer. "What's the matter, Hazelee?"

"*You* are." It busted out like a belch, but I didn't feel like saying excuse me. "You've been home since Wednesday and you've barely even talked to me."

"Oh. Well." He sat down on the porch steps and tugged at my arm, but I wouldn't budge. "It's not that I don't *want* to. There's nothing I'd like better than to take you for a ride in the pickup again. But I only have four days, and a guy has stuff to do before he ships out to the Pacific for who knows how long. Stuff that's more . . ."

"Important," I finished. Even my eyes felt hard.

"Maybe not more important, just more urgent. I had to help my dad get the bean crop in, didn't I?"

You didn't have to take Estelle out two nights in a row, I thought—but decided not to mention it. What was the use?

After a long pause, Jed tried again. "Remember the first conversation we had, a coupla years back?"

I stuck my hands in my pockets and nodded. I'd fallen out of a tree next to the gravel road and knocked myself out a little. He had come along in his pickup while I was still flat on my back, trying to figure out what made those black spots in front of my eyes. I was all right, but when he found out nobody was home at my house, he couldn't leave it at that. "We'd better make sure you're okay. How about you come along to our south field and help me pick melons?"

He probably didn't think I would be much help, but even my mother admits I'm a good worker once I get started. From that time on, Jed would often pause on the road outside our house and tap the horn to ask if I wanted to go along on a trip or a chore. Did I remember? Sure, I remembered.

"We talked about how this crazy war has shuffled everybody around," Jed was saying, "and how we all have to look out extra sharp for each other, right?"

"Uh-huh." He pitched in to help us, too, so Mom didn't mind me returning the favor as long as I kept up with my own chores. We got to be friends, or that's what I thought. Jed taught me to hoot like an owl and whistle like a thrush and tie a slipknot that never failed. I told him jokes I'd heard on the radio. And we talked—about the war, and our favorite food, and baseball, and movies, and Jed's plan to enlist in the marines as soon as he could talk his dad into it. And about Estelle.

That's when Estelle was flirting with the entire football team at Hood River High. She knew Jed, of course. He'd been our neighbor forever, but he was a few years older and never looked like a movie star, though I loved the way his eyes grinned and his hair crinkled. Then, two days after he turned twenty-one, he marched down to the marine recruiter's office and enlisted. I guess he talked his dad into it. What's more, he started talking in a more serious way to Estelle, and all of a sudden she began to see the good things about him that I'd seen all along.

"That's what I need from you, Hazelee," he was saying now. "To look after things while I'm gone. Check on my mother every now and then, and ask my dad if you could help him around the farm, and . . . cheer up your sister if she gets blue. Could you do that?"

I'd been keeping watch on the home front for three years now—what he was asking me to do just sounded like more of the same. And Estelle usually didn't need cheering up. But he was staring at me really hard, as if his eyes wanted to send a message he couldn't say out loud. I looked down, kicking at the grass. "Okay."

"That's my girl." He stuck out his hand again. "Put her there, pardner."

I stared at his hand, then knocked it aside and threw my arms around him. "I want to go, too!" Better than staying here and watching everybody else leave.

"Yeah." His voice sounded funny, maybe because I was squeezing so hard. "The marines don't know what they're missing. If I get word that they're putting together a water-balloon assault division, I'll let you know. In the meantime—" He pulled away and took a shiny silver dollar out of his pocket, holding it up for me to see. "The selective service board gave me this when I enlisted. Where I'm going, I won't need it. So you keep it for me until I get back, okay?" He put the coin in my hand. "Keep it in your pocket so you'll remember what I said about looking after things. And remember to write." The screen door slammed and he stood up quickly. "Say, beautiful! All set?"

Estelle ran down the porch steps with a sweater over one arm and her cheeks the same color as her red-checked dress. "All set!" She tweaked one of my braids with a grin. "Watch out—I'll get you back somehow."

Jed tugged the other braid. "I'm counting on you, Hazelee." He grabbed Estelle's hand and they ran to his car, giggling like kids. In the back of the sedan, Mrs. Lanski's wide red smile stretched even wider and redder. The silver dollar felt heavy in my hand. I turned it over to the side with Lady Liberty walking out of the sunrise.

In a minute the Ford roared away, and Mom started back to the house, retying her apron. Her shoulders sagged, as though talking with Mrs. Lanski had taken some of the starch out of her. "I'll never understand that woman. After all these years she refuses to admit there's a war on. She talks as if Jed's going off on a South Sea cruise." She saw me with a start, as though she'd forgotten I was there. "Let's get cracking so we'll be ready when Aunt Ruth comes."

A few minutes later I stood at the sink washing dishes while the radio played "You Are My Sunshine." But the sunshine had gone out of the day for me. A tear splashed into the dishwater, then another. I was a pilot in a Corsair fighter plane, gliding over the Pacific, spotting Japanese subs. There's another one—bombs away! Splash. Mom bustled into the kitchen, put away her dust rag, and paused by the cake she'd made for the picnic. It was shaped like a big V for *Victory*, with one side tinted red and the other white with blue letters spelling out HURRY HOME, JED. "There's a dent in the J here," she announced. "Do you happen to know who made it?"

I shrugged without turning around.

She picked up a knife and smoothed the top of the J, where a finger had been. "Better hurry. Aunt Ruth will be here any minute. And *please* change out of those sad-looking overalls. They're almost too small for you anyway."

"I'm not going to the picnic."

"Not going? Why not?"

"Don't feel like it . . . I'm tired of telling people goodbye."

Just last Wednesday we had said goodbye to my dad, who'd spent less than a week at home before going back to his wartime job in the Portland shipyards. A few months ago my brother, Frank, left to join the Young America Work Corps, and my best friend, Mary Frances, had been gone for a whole year now. The picnic looked like just another long strung-out goodbye, dressed up like a party. Just about everybody in the neighborhood would be going, but I didn't care. Half the community's sugar ration would be on the table in a cake or a pie or a tall pitcher of lemonade, but I didn't care. There would be sack races and fifty-yard dashes that I could have won—easy— but I didn't care.

After a pause, Mom said in her no-nonsense victory voice,

"Now, Hazel. This war's been hard on everybody and I know you miss your father and Frank. I do, too." Forks and knives clattered as she gathered them up from the table and dropped them into the dishwater. "I'm sure your father would like to stay home and tend his apple trees instead of building ships. I'm sure Frank would like to start school with you on Monday instead of pounding nails." I wasn't so sure myself—his letters sounded like he was having a great time. "But our country needs them more. We all have to do our part—"

I turned around, finally. "What part am I not doing if I don't go to a picnic?"

Mom was buttoning her suit jacket while a little crease appeared between her eyes. "I was getting to that. Jed needs all of our support. What will he think if you don't show up to wish him well?"

"I already did. Besides, he won't miss me as long as Estelle's around."

"Oh, Hazel, don't be silly." She adjusted the victory pin on her jacket. Not even my mother usually wore a suit to a picnic, but she was chairman of the Citizens' League and they were setting up a table to sell war bonds. "What do you propose to do all afternoon? Besides sulk?"

"Go bird-watching."

"Again?" Mom put one hand on her hip and the crease between her eyes deepened. She knew it wasn't birds I was watching for. "I think you could find a more worthwhile—" We heard a swish of gravel on the drive and a blast from the horn. Mom picked up the cake. "This is your last chance. Are you coming or not?"

"No. I mean, no, ma'am."

"You'll regret it after Jed's gone."

I just shook my head. For a minute Mom looked like she might drag me out to Aunt Ruth's car by my overall straps. But then she said, "Have it your way, Miss Stubborn. Just stay out of trouble. We'll be back before dark."

After the last bowl went into the drainer, I tipped the water out of the dishpan, watching as the drain sucked it down and made a burp. In the stillness that followed, the clock in the living room ticked louder and louder, like a heartbeat.

I threw down the dishrag and ran to the bedroom, where a pair of binoculars hung from my bedpost. They belonged to Frank, really, but he was letting me use them. Not that he *knew* he was letting me use them, but he must have meant for me to, since he didn't take them along when he joined the Young America Corps. I poked them into my knapsack along with a notebook and pencil. Then I ran out the back way, letting the screen door slam like I wasn't supposed to.

2

HAWK'S NEST

The cidery air shot into my lungs and burst out in a shout. I charged the rows of fruit trees lined up like soldiers on drill, dodging the support props and windfall apples—watch out for land mines, men!

Then my foot came right down on a Golden Delicious that must have been lying there for a week. "Yeechhh!" I scraped off my saddle oxford and trotted on toward the stretch of woods that divided our orchard from the Lanski property.

The Lanskis were our closest neighbors, but except for Jed they kept to themselves, mostly. Mrs. Lanski was "poorly" and her husband tended her when he wasn't tending his farm. He came over sometimes to see my parents on farm or neighbor business, but he'd never spoken to me—except once.

That was almost three years ago, when my brother decided that the round hill sticking up like a bent knee from the edge of the Lanski property would be a perfect observation post for the Hood River Junior Auxiliary Air Patrol (or HRJAAP). He had let me tag along when he walked up the gravel road to our neighbors' house and knocked on their front door.

"You want to do *what*?" Mr. Lanski demanded after stepping out on the porch and closing the front door behind him.

"Watch for enemy planes, sir. Your hill is the highest point for miles around."

"Nuts!" I got the idea Mr. Lanski could have said worse.

That wasn't what Frank expected, but he held his ground. He'd worn his Scout uniform to make a better impression and I, for one, was pretty impressed. "It's not nuts, sir. We've been attacked and every American must do his part to protect the mainland. Who knows where the Japanese will strike next? They're diabolical, sir. They could be spying on us this very—"

Mr. Lanski held up a hand and turned to me. "You're his sister, right?"

This close, he looked as big and craggy as a rock cliff. All I could do was nod. He turned back to Frank.

"Okay. *You* can go up there, and this little girl, so long as you stay on the hill. But nobody else. I don't favor being overrun with nosy kids. Understand?"

Frank had to promise, on Scout's honor. He was disappointed by the terms, though—he'd wanted to recruit his whole troop into the HRJAAP. Since he couldn't go back on his word, the only other member was me. Funny to think that I owed it to Mr. Lanski, who didn't seem to know patriotic duty from a hole in the ground.

The hill began just beyond the woods. With a cheer I charged it like Teddy Roosevelt, zigzagging on the switchbacks, crashing through the scrub oak and collapsing, winded, on the bald top that Frank dubbed "Hawk's Nest."

The quietness began to sneak up again, making me think about lemonade and cupcakes and sack races. Would anybody be missing me at the park? Probably not. And anyway, it was just a dumb picnic. Except at the end, when the women would be hugging Jed with their faces all twisted up and the men would be shaking his hand and talking in big hearty voices even though everybody knew that he might never—

I jumped up, threw off the knapsack, and ran twice around the top of the hill, fast as I could go. Then I slid to a halt beside the flag that Frank and I had made. It was tacked on a staff as high as my shoulder. Clapping a hand over my heart, I began rattling off, "I pledge allegiance to the flag of the United States of America—"

But it didn't help. The thought I was trying to keep from

thinking caught up with "liberty and justice for all": Jed might never come back. Never. Like Bobby Hedgecock, who was buried in Italy, or Lyndon Reynolds, at the bottom of the Pacific. Never never never.

A breeze lifted the flag, rolling out the words Frank had marked with a laundry pen on one of the crooked white stripes: *Remember Pearl Harbor.* They'd faded a lot, but I could still read them. I sank down on my knees and took three deep breaths.

The main thing I remembered about Pearl Harbor was what didn't happen. December 7, 1941, was my ninth birthday. Our family was supposed to drive down to Hood River that afternoon for dinner at Grandma Anderson's: all my favorite food, plus presents from the aunts and uncles. The news we heard that morning didn't change the plan, but everybody who came to Grandma's was so worried about war with Japan that the party felt like a funeral. Except for the presents, of course.

The best part of that day, for me, was unwrapping the roller skates I'd been begging for since June. Daddy helped me lace them up, then went outside to watch me try them out. "Say! Look at Hazel go!" he shouted with real surprise. (Frank had never caught on to skating and Estelle never tried.) I rolled down Grandma's drive and turned onto the sidewalk, and since Daddy didn't say any more, I figured he was speechless with amazement. At the edge of Grandma's lot I made a turn, with my arms spread out: ta da! But Daddy wasn't there. He'd gone back into the house to listen to the radio.

The metal wheels made a scritchy sound on the concrete. I skated around the block, pretending to be Sonja Henie. Then I did it again. Then again, and again, until I lost count. By the time anybody remembered I was out there, the red winter sun had dropped behind Grandma's house and I couldn't feel my nose.

Daddy apologized for the lousy birthday, but Frank told me to buck up and take it like a Scout. "Face the facts, Nut," he explained, looking very serious. (And usually I hate it when he calls me Hazel Nut, but since he was the only one who bothered to really talk to me that day, I let it go.) "You can bet your life we're at war now, and everybody's going to have to give up something. You just gave up your birthday."

I gave up a lot more than that, of course. First Daddy, who turned the orchard management over to Uncle Chet so he could help build victory ships in Portland Yard. Last year Mary Frances moved to Bremerton so that both her parents could work in a weapons plant. Early in the summer my mom finally gave in to Frank's nagging and let him join the Young America Corps. Now Jed was going, so there was hardly anybody left. And I gave up my tenth and eleventh birthdays, too, because now December 7 was a Day That Would Live in Infamy. For every "Happy Birthday" sung, I heard a dozen "God Bless America"s and at least one "You're a Sap, Mr. Jap."

All that gave me as much reason to be mad at the enemy as anybody.

I pulled the field glasses out of my knapsack and stood up to survey the area, starting north. Frank was right about the view. Our family orchard was near the high end of Hood River Valley, and from Hawk's Nest I could see almost all of it. The valley lies like a giant's arm between the blue hills, ending with the town of Hood River on its palm. The town is about ten miles away, too long a reach for my binoculars. But in my mind I could see its pointy steeples and gray warehouse roofs and the wide Columbia flowing west, flashing like a mirror and dotted with lumber barges.

Eastward lay Ash Grove, a little farm community hunkered down in furry-looking clumps of cedar and ponderosa pine. The hills and fields around it were covered with loaded apple trees, strung out in rows. The white oak staves propping up the heavy branches made the trees look like spiders, with legs poking out on every side. With September almost over we were getting close to the peak of harvest season, and my uncle Chet had passed up today's picnic to keep at it. I could see his tractor crawling between rows while the Mexican farmhands loaded the trailer with apple boxes.

Swinging the binoculars southward, I caught my breath as Mount Hood jumped into view: huge, quiet, and clear as glass against the blue sky. It was so big and sharp it reared up in the lenses like a wave that never fell. It seemed to me that a signal tower on that peak would be high enough to radio halfway across the Pacific. That's why I always searched the north side of the mountain so closely. But I never found anything and was starting to wonder if I ever would.

For a while after Pearl Harbor, everybody was looking up into the sky, expecting the Japs to bomb Seattle or San Francisco any day. But that was three years ago, almost. Some people were less excited than they used to be about collecting scrap and saving gasoline, and even Frank lost interest in the HRJAAP after a year. He said I could recruit Mary Frances to help me watch on Saturday afternoons, so I had company for a while. After she moved, it was a lonely duty, and sometimes I was tempted to give it up. But as long as American boys were going off to fight in the Pacific, I would stick to my post. All the more reason to now, since Jed had asked me to watch out for things.

I felt for his silver dollar in my pocket, remembering that he'd also asked me to look in on his mother and help his dad. The idea made my stomach quiver, because I barely knew her and didn't like the little I knew of him. Unlike our family and most of the neighbors, Mr. Lanski grew row crops, not apples, and was busy year-round with his potatoes or strawberries or asparagus. But he was contrary enough to like working alone— maybe I could offer to help once or twice, and he'd refuse, and that would be that. Mrs. Lanski was a little scary to me, but for Jed's sake I'd try to visit her once a month, starting in October. In the meantime, I'd keep an eye on things from here.

A movement flickered in the Lanskis' yard, a quarter mile

away, half hidden by white oaks. Up went the field glasses again—but all I could see was clothes flapping on the line and the maid taking them down. She was dressed in her usual outfit: loose dungarees rolled up at the ankles and a floppy sunbonnet that hid her face. Mr. Lanski refused to hire any farm help, but his wife had to have a maid—from Mexico, Jed told us—on account of her condition. "I know what her 'condition' is," Mom said later with a sniff. "It's called laziness."

The maid was the only suspicious activity in sight, so I watched until she went back to the house with her laundry basket. Then I sat down and flopped on my back and gazed up at the puffy clouds drifting across the sky like sailboats. The flag sighed in the breeze and my eyelids drooped. It was nice up here, where not much changed and nobody ever had to say goodbye. . . .

A gust of wind snapped the flag against the pole, like my mother slapping our bedroom wall: rise and shine! I sat up and stretched, then took another look over the valley with my field glasses. An airplane engine whined from far away, just a moving dot in my lenses. When it blurred out of sight, I flipped open my notebook and wrote *Sat., September 23, 1944, 2:47 p.m.* I checked the time by the watch Daddy had brought from Portland. An early present for my twelfth birthday, he said: "You'll have to put in some extra hours in the orchard with Frank gone. This'll help you keep track."

Partly cloudy [I wrote], *wind NW about 10 mph. About 1:10 p.m.*

spotted two Jap Zero planes headed NE. Radio'd hq but no sound. Crawled through brush following radio wire. Reached bottom of hill, found wire cut! Climbed back uphill to get supplies—one of the Zero planes circled around and spotted me. R'chd knapsack under fire, grabbed sack, and raced downhill. Fixed wire w/ solder and a cigarette lighter. Climbed back up using diversionary manuvers and reached radio, wh. I fortunately left under cover. Radio'd hq with message. Dodged fire from Zero until P51-D Mustang apprd and shot Jap plane out of the sky. Pilot to me: Who's down there? You just saved Bonneville Dam. Me to plt: An American citizen, doing my part. Plt wagged wings in salute.

When I read it over, I could almost hear the machine-gun rattle and the crackle of radio static. The last thing I wrote was *s.n.* for "situation normal."

If you read a year's worth of my surveillance reports, you'd think it was a miracle I was still alive.

A little later I stuffed the field glasses into my knapsack and started home, humming "Anchors Aweigh." Halfway down the hill, a flash of white in the bushes caught my eye. Better check it out, I told myself. Can't be too careful.

The whiteness was a ragged strip of paper about an inch wide and four inches long, flapping in the wind like a trapped bird. A thread was tied to one end. I untangled the thread from the twigs and slowly pulled the paper free. The ink had faded, but when I smoothed it out for a good look, the marks were sharp enough to send little needle pricks through my brain.

The writing was in Japanese.

3

THE RIDDLE IN THE BRUSH

Breathless, I tore into the house and headed straight for Frank's room, which opened off the kitchen. Under his bed was a box, and I was pretty sure that's where I'd find what I was looking for.

A few months after Pearl, Frank had seen an advertisement in *Boys' Life* magazine: "Know Your Enemy!" He'd worked extra chores to earn the money to buy a "complete course, which will teach you basic proficiency in the Japanese language in one easy lesson per day!"

It wasn't that easy. For one thing, the Japanese used three

different alphabets and mixed them up whenever they felt like it. "Sneaky devils," Frank muttered. "Straight-talking Yanks would never come up with a system like this."

The most difficult alphabet was called kanji, because it used symbols to mean whole words. *Kanji was developed from the Chinese system of writing,* we read in lesson one. *Though the characters are similar in form, they differ in meaning from the Chinese. Kanji includes about 10,000 characters, but you should be able to conduct basic transactions with no more than 600.*

"Six *hundred*!" I yelled when Frank read that. "How are we going to get six hundred characters learned before we're attacked again?"

Frank flipped ahead in the book. "It looks like 'basic transactions' means making hotel reservations and asking directions. Like Jap spies are going to ask where the munitions plants are."

We almost gave up right there but kept on through three and a half not-so-easy lessons. We learned to say "Please excuse me," "Good afternoon," and "Thank you very much."

"That'll help if we run into *polite* spies," Frank grumbled, but by then he was already saving money for a signal lamp, complete with five easy lessons in Morse code. The language course went into the box with his other old projects.

After finding it, I had to brush off bits of glue and sawdust before turning to the list of "Common Kanji Characters" in the back. They were figures made of dots and tiny, knife-blade slashes. At first glance it was hard to make out the differences between characters—my eyes shifted back and forth so fast they almost rattled. I pushed my bangs back and tucked my feet up with a big sigh. To my mind, the kanji symbols looked as alike as the Japanese themselves.

A few hundred Japanese people used to live in the valley. I would see them on Saturdays in town: small men and women with straight black hair and tilted eyes, buying feed at the farm supply or hauling black-eyed babies down Portland Avenue. Some belonged to the Apple Growers' Association, and I could remember Daddy saying that nobody worked harder. They mostly kept to themselves, though. They had their own clubs, their own picnics, their own churches. When I went to grammar school in Ash Grove in first and second grade, there was a girl named Yuri and her little brother, Chiho. Yuri was so shy she never talked much, and I was shy around her, too. She and her brother were so small, with round faces as flat as plates and eyes as black as shoe buttons, that they didn't seem all the way real. More like dolls. Frank knew some Japanese kids in Dee, where his school was. He even palled around a little with Tom and Lewis Miasako. Their last name sounded like a comic book word to me: *socko!*

One afternoon, early in the war, Frank stomped into the house with a swollen lip and a bruise under one eye. "Jeepers, bud!" Daddy greeted him in the kitchen (this was before Daddy moved to Portland). "Did you get the number of that truck?"

"Got in a fight."

"Oh, Frank." Mom sighed while she chopped onions for meat loaf. "There's a much better way to settle your differences than—"

"It wasn't just me. It was me and Claude Roberts and a coupla other guys against the Miasakos and their Jap friends."

After a brief pause, Daddy said, "I think we can let the boys in uniform fight this one out, son."

"You don't get it, Dad. Tom and Lew have a shortwave radio they won't give up. The law says they have to, but they're hiding—"

"Let the law handle it, Frank."

"What if the law doesn't? What if they're sending messages right now to Hirohito, and—"

"Don't be silly," Mom said with a laugh that sounded a little wobbly. "Two schoolboys sending secrets to the emperor of Japan? And what kind of 'secrets' would they know, anyway?"

Frank folded his arms and stuck out his chin. "You never can tell. Claude says Japs are sneakier than the Germans."

"Claude doesn't know any more than you do," Daddy said. "If the Miasakos are breaking the law, the U.S. government will take care of it. It's no business of yours."

"Yes, sir," Frank muttered. For a while the kitchen was silent, except for lard popping in the skillet and the knife crunching down on onions. Frank looked angry, Mom looked worried, and Daddy looked sad. I remember feeling scared, but I couldn't say why.

The U.S. government took care of it, just like Daddy said. When spring came, Tom and Lew Miasako disappeared, along with Yuri and Chiho and all their people. The Japanese signs in store windows came down and no more high chattery voices could be heard downtown on Saturday afternoons. They had been sent to camp.

I'd always wanted to go to camp, like Frank used to with the Scouts. But this was for wartime security, not fun. Mom said it was a shame the Japanese had to leave their homes and property, but Daddy didn't say much, just kept looking sad.

By then I knew why: trained machinists were needed to build ships and planes and missiles, and he was one. He spent the winter arranging things with Uncle Chet and getting all the farm equipment in tip-top shape, and in April we all went down to Hood River station to see him off. Changes were coming thick and fast by then. Our Buick sedan went up on blocks so we could save gasoline and tire rubber. Mom volunteered for the ration board and the Citizens' League, and Estelle for the Red Cross. Frank started the HRJAAP and I outgrew my new roller skates. Before long I forgot all about the Hood River Japanese.

But finding that message tangled in the bushes had brought them to mind again, and how! I couldn't tell how old the paper was, but it couldn't have lasted all the way through a wet, frosty winter. Less than six months, then. Had some of the Japanese escaped from camp? Were they setting up an outpost, getting ready for an invasion? Or could it be that the invasion was under way and the enemy had landed and were leaving messages to let their countrymen know what they were up to?

The more I thought about it, the more I realized this was the most exciting thing that had ever happened to me.

Mom brought some cold fried chicken and a square of victory cake home from the picnic and made me eat it in the kitchen like a civilized child while she put together a macaroni salad for Sunday dinner. "We made one hundred seventy-five dollars from bond sales! Not bad for a Saturday afternoon."

Her smile looked like it was painted on and her voice sounded a little too cheerful. That worry crease remained between her eyes. I knew why, and felt a little guilty because three whole hours had passed without me thinking about Jed. Still, after wolfing down the food, I excused myself and made a beeline for the Japanese book hidden under my pillow.

When the Lanskis' Ford pulled up in our drive, I was still flipping pages and comparing characters to the marks on my secret message. Sometime later, the Ford backed away and Estelle got into a long teary conversation with Mom in the living room. Finally she came to bed, sniffling, and it was impossible to concentrate on language study after that, because of remembering that neither of us would see Jed for a while.

I didn't have much to show for my hours of work, either. All I knew was that one of the characters on the message might mean "mother." Or it might not. It stood to reason sneaky Japs would have a sneaky language—maybe it was too much for me. Maybe tomorrow, when we went down to Hood River for Sunday dinner at Grandma's, I should run to the police station and turn over the evidence.

Sunday morning clouded up and rained and so did Estelle. The only advantage was that I didn't have to fight anybody for the Sunday paper. I went right to the front page, looking for any report of suspicious activity or mysterious messages found in Oregon. No luck, though. President Roosevelt would be giving a radio message on Monday, American troops were plowing through France, the nation's schoolchildren were doing their part with a massive scrap-metal collection at the beginning of the fall semester—just like they did every year.

After paging through section one, I spread out the comics. "Little Orphan Annie" used to be my favorite, but lately I was going straight to "Terry and the Pirates." I'd even started cutting out episodes to keep and read again. Not that Annie wasn't doing her part: every week she was on the trail of a Nazi spy or German sabotage. But her Junior Commando Club was for babies. The best a Junior Commando could do for the war effort was drink her Ovaltine.

Terry Lee was the real thing: he'd roamed the Far East since he was a boy, hunting for his grandfather's treasure with his pals Pat Ryan and George Webster Confucius, a Chinese servant they called Connie. When the war broke out, Terry enlisted in the army air corps, but because of his knowledge of Orientals and their ways he often parachuted behind enemy lines. In the current story, Terry had broken into a Chinese spy ring and won the confidence of Chan Sung, their leader. Now Chan Sung and his gang were helping the Allies to intercept Japanese code messages. Today Terry had captured a Japanese sailor, who might have been a spy! My eyes raced over the strip.

> CHAN SUNG: He lies, boss! He is a spy! He cally message
> in seclet code!
> TERRY: Don't damage him, fellows! He may be a
> valuable source of information!
> CHAN SUNG: (to Jap) Speak! Where you flom? Where
> you go?
> TERRY: Hold on, Chan! (to Jap) May as well talk now,
> Nippon-san, or we'll have to make you talk!
> JAP: Me just poor worthless sailor! Know nothing!

It might take all week for the prisoner to break down, but he would sooner or later. Japs acted tough but were cowards at heart—everybody knew that, not just from the comics but also from posters and movie cartoons. They were small, with buckteeth and thick eyeglasses. You could tell them from other Orientals because of the space between their big toe and the other toes, caused by the sandals they wore.

"Hazel!" Mom stood in the kitchen doorway, drying her hands on a dish towel. "What are you doing, lying around in your pajamas? Get dressed for church, right now!"

I was having second thoughts about going to the police. Before turning over the message, maybe I should try harder to translate it. If Terry Lee could worm an answer out of a Japanese prisoner, I ought to be able to crack this code. Especially since I had a codebook.

On Monday morning, Estelle pounced on me with a water pistol when I came out of the bathroom—payback for balloon-bombing her. Nothing could keep her down for long; she was like a beach ball, always slipping out of your arms to bob up to the surface. Not that I wanted her to mope around until Jed came back, but getting a stream of water right in the eye felt like too much high spirits. It blinded me, so I knocked over the lamp table while chasing her.

By the time we got everything sorted out, I was late for school and Estelle would have to hustle to catch her ride to Hood River, where she worked at Northwest Bank. We left the house together, and at the end of the drive she paused to slip a letter to Jed in the mailbox. "Can you keep a secret?"

"Sure."

"Jed and I are engaged."

"*What?*" I felt like I'd been ambushed again. "Last May you were engaged to Orville Castle!"

"Orville and I broke up six months ago, silly."

"But you've only been going with Jed since June. And most of that time he was away at basic training."

"I've known him all my life."

"But—"

"Not like a boyfriend, I admit. But it's good to be just friends before you decide you're in love."

Huh. Jed and I were better friends than he'd ever been with Estelle, but it wasn't likely Jed would decide he was in love with *me*. Or not anytime soon. I wasn't even sure that I wanted him to be; it's just that next to Estelle, I felt plain as a stick. She was honey-colored curls and flirty blue eyes. I was straight brown hair, straight brown eyebrows, and bangs. But all I could think to say was, "You're only eighteen."

"Now you sound like Mom." We paused at the bend in the road. "Mom says I have to wait till I'm twenty to get married. But I'll talk her into it by the time Jed comes home, you watch. In the meantime, zip your lip. Have a good day, Hazelkins."

When Estelle smiled, it was hard to stay mad at her. I just heaved a big sigh, got a better grip on my book satchel, and walked down the road to the shortcut that led to school.

4

OUR OWN WAR HERO

When gas rationing started, the school board decided it would be more efficient to reopen the old one-room school-house in our neighborhood than run a bus to Hood River every day. It would have been a good idea, except for the problem of keeping a teacher.

The first was a nervous, middle-aged man who smelled to me like overripe apples and sometimes had trouble getting his words out. One night I overheard Mom telling Daddy about the teacher's "problem with the bottle," but by the time I figured out what the problem was, he was gone. Miss Golightly took his place and spent the rest of the term teaching us how to play contract bridge, with one kid always standing sentry in case anyone from the school board showed up. We would have given half a year's sugar ration to have her back, but Miss Golightly married a soldier and moved to Los Angeles.

Last year it was Mrs. Wahl, who almost quit after Owen Erickson put a dead rattlesnake in her lunch bucket. She spent the rest of the year making speeches about perseverance, but at closing day exercises she let us know she wouldn't be back.

As secretary of the school board, my mother spent all of August and most of September writing letters and running up long-distance charges on the telephone. School had already started for most of the nation's youth when she walked into the kitchen one afternoon, waving a letter and shouting, "Victory!" She wouldn't tell me any details, except to say that the new teacher had been talked out of retirement. That sounded like an old lady with high-button shoes who would drill us on times tables and make us memorize "Excelsior" and "Breathes there the man with soul so dead."

Still, I would have been looking forward to the first day of school if the other business wasn't so heavy on my mind. As I followed the path through the woods, the hemlocks and white oak trees leaned over me, muttering that maybe it had been a mistake not to go to the police on Sunday. Suppose whoever had left that slip of paper in the rhododendrons was lurking behind one of those trees, watching me pass? I felt my mouth going dry at the thought. Terry Lee often found himself in situations like this—what would he do? Stay alert, for sure. Know your enemy!

A couple of times I heard noises and stopped to listen so hard I could feel the hairs on my arms stand up. Then I'd start walking again, telling myself not to run because if anybody was watching, I couldn't let him know I was scared. Still, I couldn't keep my steps from speeding up, little by little, as the dry leaves on the forest floor whispered "Hurry! Hurry!"

The path to the schoolhouse was only half a mile long, but it felt like ten. My heart was thumping faster than a hare's hind leg when the schoolhouse, bright with a fresh coat of white paint, finally sprang up at the end of the path. To me it looked like an angel with open arms.

I pounded up the steps and pushed the door. At the squeal of hinges everybody turned to look: Marvin Peters, Owen and Jackie Erickson, Roger and Margie Holmes, Sherman Schultz, Ivy and Gladys Thompson, Petilia, Maria, and little Susie Lopez. All present now that I'd showed up, ten minutes late. "And who is this?" came a voice from the front of the room. It was a man's voice—not an old man's, either.

When my eyes adjusted to the dimness, I saw him, in a khaki shirt and dark olive trousers, standing behind the desk. A service pin gleamed on his collar. His dark hair was thinning on top, but his eyes seemed to penetrate, like Terry's, under strong black eyebrows. His jaw was square and firm. This was the teacher the school board had talked out of retirement? Nobody

retired from the service with a war on, unless by honorable discharge. I felt my jaw drop.

"Does your name happen to be Hazel Anderson, little girl?"

I swallowed. "Yes, sir." Since he was one of our brave boys in
uniform, I could forgive him for the "little girl."

"Then take a seat, Hazel. I'm Corporal Arthur Mayhew. I
was just telling the class a little about myself." I found my old
seat between Ivy and Gladys while he went on to tell about
dropping out of college after Pearl Harbor to enlist. After a
year on Guadalcanal and the Solomon Islands he'd received
an honorable discharge but served another year as a combat
instructor at Fort Lewis. When he heard about this teaching
position he jumped at it, because he was studying to be a
teacher when the war interrupted his plans. Though duty might
call him back to active service, after today he would not wear his
uniform, and he preferred we call him Mr. Mayhew instead of
Corporal.

Owen stuck up his hand. "Could I please be excused, Mr.
Mayhew?"

The teacher blinked in surprise. "What for?"

"I have to . . . you know." The class tittered, while Mr. Mayhew looked like he might be deciding whether Owen really had
to or not. But then he nodded. We all glanced at each other as
Owen left the building. He pulled the same trick with every
new teacher, but surely he wouldn't dare try it with this one.
Somebody should warn Mr. Mayhew, I thought. Nobody did,

even though Marvin and Roger were nudging each other and Margie was sitting up straight with an expression like she'd just swallowed a fly. The teacher started a speech about what he wanted to accomplish during this school year, but nobody was listening. "As you can guess, I haven't had much classroom experience, so we can learn together. Think of it as an adventure—"

POW! came the first blast. Then pow-pow-pow-pow! in a chain. Owen rushed in, panting. "It's the Japs! We're surrounded!"

All eyes went to the teacher's desk. Mr. Mayhew had disappeared.

My heart was flopping like a fish: What if Owen was right this time and the Japs had invaded and shot Mr. Mayhew through the window! What if the whole plan was written on that message I had decided not to take to the police! For a minute I felt like I was choking—but then a hand crept over the top of the teacher's desk, followed by Mr. Mayhew himself. His lips looked gray and his forehead shone with cold sweat.

Nobody laughed. Owen looked like he'd rather be on Guadalcanal.

"Come here, boy." The teacher's voice grated like a buzz saw as he stood up and walked around to the front of the desk—no, limped, favoring his left leg. "See this?" He slapped the leg. "I took a piece of shrapnel right below the knee and when the medics got to me, there wasn't much left. They put my leg together again, but I'll never win a footrace. That's why I got the discharge. I can't chase you down and turn you over my knee, but if you try another stunt like that, I'll find somebody who can, even if it's the mayor. You read me?"

Owen's dad happened to *be* the mayor, but his face was as bright as a fire engine as he shuffled back to his seat. Now that the shock was over, I felt like dancing on my desk. This was too good to be true: a war hero for a teacher! For the next eight months he could teach me anything—fractions, principal rivers, chief agricultural products of Mongolia—and I'd lap it up like strawberries and cream. He even dismissed school early. The first day had probably taken a lot out of him, seeing as how he was still building up his strength.

Owen had a lot to answer for, and he was answering for it as hard as he could while Marvin and Roger shoved him around the school yard. Usually it was the other way around, but Owen wasn't shoving back this time. He must have felt like he deserved it, a little. "Hey! I hadda—stop it! I hadda find out if he's really seen action—you want a bloody nose, Marv?"

Ivy Thompson couldn't get over Mr. Mayhew's dark, deepset eyes. "They look absolutely *haunted,* don't you think?" She and Margie were making plans to combine their sugar rations and bake cookies for him. "Come join us, Hazel," Margie begged. "We need your help." I knew what that meant: We need your sugar. At fourteen, Margie was the oldest student in school except for Marvin, and the bossiest, but I wasn't having any. "No, thanks!" I called over my shoulder, and trotted off toward the path.

My plans had changed: first I'd scout the hill and the woods all around to see if there were any more messages. Then I'd turn them over to Mr. Mayhew, maybe with another word or two translated. I pictured his eyes shining when he said, "With alert and quick-thinking patriots like you, Hazel Anderson, I may never have to go back to Guadalcanal."

Mom was at a meeting when I got home, but she'd left a note saying that Uncle Chet wanted me in the orchard as soon as possible. That meant no time for scouting. I could have spit. Why, when I finally made an important discovery, did it have to happen at harvest season? I took a few minutes to check the funny pages in the newspaper. Terry Lee's Japanese prisoner was still being stubborn, but I couldn't help shivering when Terry gave a command to his Chinese gang: "Search the jungle, fellows! There could be more of them!" Exactly what I'd been thinking myself!

But Uncle Chet kept me so busy that afternoon that all I had time for, once I got home, was to wash my hands and sit down at the table for dinner. "So," Mom said, briskly passing the creamed corn after saying grace. "How do you like the new teacher?"

I nearly choked on my salmon croquette, which had been sliding down easy. "You said you talked somebody out of retirement! I thought it was going to be some old lady!"

"Well, he did come out of retirement, in a way."

"Who is he?" Estelle asked. "Where's he from?"

"He's an army vet who was wounded in Guadalcanal. From Santa Barbara, California."

"That's a nice place. What's he doing in a backwater like this?"

Mom ~~~~~~~ the "backwater" but answered the question. ~~~~~~ isn't much family down there anymore and says all he wants now is peace and quiet. His experience in the Pacific was quite terrible, it seems—" She broke off, maybe because she'd just remembered that Jed was headed for the Pacific, where "quite terrible" things could happen to him, too. "Of course Mr. Mayhew knows we can't pay him much, but since he's staying with the Hedgecocks, his room and board are taken care of."

"He might re-enlist if the war goes on much longer," I said.

"It won't," Estelle said brightly. "Now that Jed's marines are on the way." She burst out singing her own version of the "Marines' Hymn": "From the halls of Hood River Hi-IGH School to the shores of Tok-yo Bay . . ."

"You might take this a little more seriously—" Mom began.

"I'm just having a little fun. Sure wish he would call, though."

"He'll call before he ships out. . . ."

My mind snapped like a rubber band back to the message tucked in my Japanese language book, and the salmon croquettes might have been chopped flannel pajamas for all I could taste them. Little did Jed know, when he asked me to watch out for things around here, what kind of "things" I would find!

After washing the dishes, I went straight to work on the translation. "Is Mr. Mayhew assigning lessons already?" Mom asked hopefully.

"No, I'm doing this on my own."

"That's the spirit." Mom didn't come far enough into the bedroom to see what I was doing on my own but went back to the armchair by the radio and took up some mending. Estelle was curled up on the sofa, writing to Jed. Which was good, because both were so involved they didn't hear me gasp a few minutes later.

I discovered the meaning of another character. No doubt about it: after flipping pages until my eyeballs ached, I was sure of the word *tree*. So how did it fit with my other word? Mother tree? Tree mothers? My mother the tree? Goose bumps wrinkled up on my arms. Finally I was making some real progress. It only made sense to keep at it a little longer.

5

ENEMY TERRITORY

At school the next day, Owen Erickson brought Mr. Mayhew a dozen biscuits in a paper bag by way of apology, and the two of them went outside to settle things man-to-man. That is, Mr. Mayhew settled it with some straight talking that made Owen look down at his feet and hunch his shoulders. Then they shook hands and came back into the schoolroom. The biscuits went on a shelf beside the cookies, apple pie, and apricot bread that the girls and their mothers had whomped up from a pile of scraped-together sugar.

After that, nobody seemed to know what to do, including

the teacher. He made us work the first lesson in our arithmetic books, then asked every student in the class to take turns reading aloud. Since we were in three different books, the reading was three stories cut apart and stuck together like a crazy quilt. He stretched it out as long as he could, then broke for lunch at eleven instead of eleven-thirty. After a long recess he made us name the continents and oceans on a globe and seemed disappointed that we all could. Mrs. Wahl had seen to that last year. Owen stuck up his hand.

"Sir, could you tell us about the Pacific? Like for geography?"

Of course Owen was really interested in war stories. We all were, but Mr. Mayhew's face seemed to darken, as though a cloud had passed overhead. "Maybe later, Owen. For now . . . I just can't."

A sigh came from the row next to me—Ivy Thompson was in love. Margie spoke up from the other side: "It's all right, sir. We can wait." We all chimed in that we would love to hear about the Pacific whenever he wanted to talk about it, and he dismissed school early. Out in the yard, Owen found himself in another shoving match: the boys were upset because they were sure Mr. Mayhew would have got around to sharing a few of his cookies if we'd given him time.

But with another sunny afternoon ahead, nobody could stay mad for long. "Holy cow!" Roger yelled before taking off for the woods. "This is the best teacher we've *ever* had!"

The next day Mr. Mayhew seemed to have a better grasp on what to do. He filled the morning with a spelling bee, memory drills, and arithmetic practice, and after lunch recess he started to read *Treasure Island* aloud. We all knew the story, from comic books if nothing else, but hearing Mr. Mayhew's version was like discovering it all over again. He didn't just read it—he almost lived it. At the exciting parts, he even stood up and paced, and his limp made him roll and list like Long John Silver on the deck of the *Hispaniola*. After the reading, he dismissed school—a good hour earlier than any of our former teachers had. "So you can help with the harvest," he said.

Sherman stuck his hand up. "My family owns the Ash Grove Grocery. We don't have anything to harvest."

"Then do something for the war effort, Sherman," the teacher said with an edge to his voice. The rest of us nodded emphatically.

"I don't remember discussing the harvest with him," Mom said when I told her why I was home so early again. "But we can use all the extra help we can get. It was thoughtful of him to consider that."

I wasn't sure if Mr. Mayhew was being thoughtful or if he just didn't know how to fill up a whole afternoon yet. "When I get done in the orchard, can I look for scrap metal in the woods?"

"*May* I," Mom corrected absently. "I suppose so, if Uncle Chet doesn't have anything else for you to do. Why don't you ask Gladys and some of the other girls to go with you next time? It would be much more fun with company, don't you think?"

"They're too busy baking stuff for the teacher." Sometimes my mother worried that I spent too much time alone. But it was years since Gladys Thompson was my friend, and now that she was twelve and interested in boys and clothes, she preferred to hang around with her older sister, Ivy, and Margie Holmes. I told myself it didn't matter; for me, friends were another luxury in short supply until the war was over, like sugar and coffee and gasoline.

My main job during harvest was to haul water out to the pickers and cull the bad apples they'd picked. Then I had to finish off any low branches Uncle Chet had saved for me and drive the tractor between rows while the hired hands loaded boxes on the trailer. The first few times I drove our old red Farmall it was fun, sitting way up high on that big sputtering machine. But now it was just boring. Uncle Chet throttled the engine all the way down to a crawl so the men could keep up, and the hardest thing about driving was paying enough attention not to steer into a tree.

That Wednesday and Thursday we worked until sundown, which didn't leave me any time for scouting, and after dinner I was so tired I fell asleep over the Japanese book. It helped a little to know that Terry Lee was having his problems, too: his ally Chan Sung had disappeared while searching the jungle, and the Jap sailor was still refusing to talk.

On Thursday night Jed called to say that his unit was shipping out the very next day. He only had a few minutes on the phone and didn't ask to talk to me. He passed on a message, though: So long, pardner, and remember to keep an eye on things for me.

Finally, on Friday, Uncle Chet let me off two whole hours early. "Still hunting scrap metal? Here's some to get you started." He tossed me two quarters. I couldn't help skipping most of the way home, with the money in my pocket and a whole weekend opening up, blue and sunny.

The air smelled sharp, with a tang of apples and a smudge of wood smoke. Before long the winter rains would come muscling in from the coast, so I had to make the most of this good weather. I stopped at the house long enough to grab my knapsack and field glasses and yell out where I was going. Mom yelled back: "Be sure you get home before—" I didn't catch the last words. Before dark, probably.

On the way to the hill, I started my search, making wide swings on both sides of the path with an eye peeled for papers fluttering in the brush. While climbing up to Hawk's Nest, I paused every twenty yards or so and swept the slope with my field glasses. Jed would be proud. My mind had started to keep an eye on him, too: in my imagination, I stowed away on his troop ship and headed out into the Pacific. Thanks to the movies, I knew some good places to hide on a ship, like in the lifeboats. When they arrived at their destination and it was too

late to send me back, I'd make myself known—maybe just to
Jed. Maybe I would conceal myself in the jungle and be a spy; I
hadn't worked that part out yet. One thing for sure, though: by
the time his service was up, Jed would realize that I was a *lot*
more useful to him than Estelle.

On Hawk's Nest, I dropped to my knees, holding the
binoculars at a steady angle and turning slowly to keep the
lenses from flashing. With possible enemy action in the neighborhood, I couldn't be too careful. But an engine drone from
overhead made me snap them up to the sky: a fighter plane! I
whipped out my logbook and wrote, *Fri., Sept. 29, 3:44 p.m. Corsair,
#20, sighted about 45 deg. E, headed NW.* Then a thought hit me so
hard it stopped my pencil: could it be that somebody besides
me was on alert for suspicious activity?

I jumped up to my feet. Maybe the Japanese message,
tucked inside the language book in my knapsack, was getting
too hot to hold. If the U.S. military had reason to be looking
in our bushes, I couldn't hold on to valuable information.
Meaning that if I was going to find anything more, it would
have to be today. Peering through the field glasses, I made a
slow sweep all the way around the hilltop. Not for the first
time, I wished that Frank and I had finished that observation
tower he'd wanted to build. He'd gone so far as to draw up a
plan and recruit me to help him transport a load of two-by-
twos, but then his enthusiasm died. Toting the lumber from
our garage to Hawk's Nest was so much work we never

bothered to carry it down—it was still stacked under the spruce trees.

But at least I could search closer to hand. I picked up the knapsack and took a deep breath before starting down the other side of the hill—the very thing Frank had promised Mr. Lanski we wouldn't do. But I was sure our neighbor would forgive my trespassing if he knew my mission.

His side of the hill was steeper than our side, with no path. I had to make my own, slipping between the scrubby evergreens that choked the slope. Frank would have been impressed—my progress was so stealthy not even *I* knew where I was once I'd reached the bottom of the hill.

In front of me was an orchard of gnarly old trees gone to ruin. A crop of wormy apples littered the ground, mashing to a sour-smelling pulp under my shoes. Stacks of brush were piled up below the trees, surrounded by stubble.

Then I heard a sound: Chop. Chop. Chop. A long pause, then chop-chop-chop again. It seemed to be coming from the south. Mr. Lanski's fields were mostly to the north—what reason would he have to come up this way? Chop. Chop. Keep close, men, I told my squad. We'll have a look-see. I crept out of the brush, glancing down—and choked off a gasp of surprise. The cleared ground was pocked with footprints, and they couldn't have been Mr. Lanski's. He was tall, with feet to match. These prints were small, and they ran everywhere.

The chopping noise started again, and by now I recognized

the sound of a hatchet cutting brush. Or a machete? For the first time I felt a strong urge to turn around. So strong, in fact, that I almost did. Somebody besides me occupied this space; maybe more than one body. What if I was surrounded already?

My heart hammered and my toes twitched, but somehow I kept moving forward, rolling my weight from heel to toe and pausing now and then to listen. Only the thought of an award ceremony at the White House kept me going. Thank you, Mr. President, but I only did what any loyal American . . .

Swish. Chop-chop-chop. Coming closer, I dropped to my hands and knees and slithered through the bushes. Peering through the lacy branches of a cedar shrub, I made out a pile of brush directly in front of me. Just beyond that, in the clear space, a single figure was tossing branches in a pile. His back was turned to me, and through my peephole in the branches I couldn't see his head. From the back it looked like a boy dressed in faded dungarees rolled up at the ankles. Then he bent over to whack at the brush some more and I could see the floppy sunbonnet. . . . A *sun*bonnet? Was Mr. Lanski using the maid for farmwork as well as housework?

The stack of brush at her feet was already knee-high. She picked it up and turned toward the bigger pile directly in front of me. I crouched lower and squinted through the cedar limbs.

Next minute, I found myself looking right into the flat face and slant eyes of a Jap!

I went hollow, like a straw slurping up the last of an ice

cream soda. Then I jumped to my feet—a stupid thing to do because now the Jap could see me plain as day. For a minute he looked the way I felt, with his mouth open and eyes so round the whites showed. A strange cry came out of him: "Way-missee!"

That did it. I crashed through the bushes and took off running. The enemy was right behind, with a hatchet in his hand. His face burned into my brain as I dodged the evil old trees with their branches stretching out to grab me.

But I couldn't shake him! However fast I tripped and stumbled and plunged, he was right behind, hollering, "Way! Way!"—a sharp word that bit into my ears. He was gaining—he was almost on me! This was the worst nightmare I'd ever had, and it was real!

My breath came hard as a fist. My ribs ached and my knees burned. I couldn't keep this up much longer, I couldn't—

Bam! I ran smack-dab into a tree.

6

AN INVITATION TO TEA

But a tree didn't have this much give to it or a voice that said, "Hold on, little girl, hold on. Settle down now, settle down."

Hands grabbed and held my shoulders while a voice kept talking until I understood, first, that it was speaking English, and second, that it belonged to Mr. Lanski. ". . . all right, nobody's going to hurt you. Give me a chance, I'll explain everything. . . ."

All this time a dry, sobbing sound went on in the background, which frightened me even more until I realized that I was the one making it. Get a grip on yourself, Mom would say. So I got a grip and dared another look at the Jap. He was only a few yards away, with the hatchet in his hand and that silly yellow sunbonnet shoved back on his head. In a flash I saw the whole picture: this was the Lanskis' "maid." They had been harboring one of the enemy! I caught a breath and felt it fill my lungs like fire, then whirled back to Mr. Lanski. "Traitor!"

"Now just a minute there, little girl. I said I could explain—"

"I am *not* a little girl! I'm Hazel Nell Anderson!"

"That's right, I just forgot." To my surprise, he was trying to smile. "Good to see you again, Hazel. This is Sogoji. He was just helping me get a start on replanting the orchard here."

The "maid" was smiling, too, sort of. His lips twitched nervously, like a pair of moth wings. Seen this close, he wasn't any more than a boy, with a round face, rounded shoulders, and small hands, which he didn't know what to do with. He put them together with the ax handle between, then shifted the handle from left to right and finally stuck out one hand. "I am honor' to meet Miss Hazel." At the sound of his chirpy voice, I realized what he'd been calling after me: "Wait, missy!"

I didn't take the hand he held out. By now I was furious instead of scared and spun around to Mr. Lanski again. "What's a Jap doing here?"

"Sogoji is an American."

"How can you say that? *Look* at him!"

"Because he was born here, that's how I can say that!" The

usual sour look flashed across his face, then he tried to smile again. "Let's all three sit down and talk it over, okay? Sogoji, it might be a good idea for you to put down the hatchet." He squatted on his heels, and the Jap did, too.

I stayed on my feet—easier to run if I had to. "First off," Mr. Lanski began, "you might tell me why you're trespassing."

Like Terry Lee captured by the Dragon Lady's band, I squared my shoulders and stuck out my chin and silently vowed to say nothing. Or nothing that he didn't already know. "You told us—my brother and me—that we could use the hill for air-craft observation."

"This ain't the hill," he pointed out.

"I heard a noise and figured it was my duty to check it out. There's still a war on, you know."

"Yeah," he said dryly. "I know. All right, Hazel. The truth is, we've got a little secret here." (Looks like a big one to *me*, I thought. My eyes strayed to the little secret's feet to see if there was a space between his toes, but he was wearing Western-style shoes that were so old his socks peeped through the split seams.) "Sogoji's folks, the Mitsumis, used to own a little farm south of here. But Mrs. Mitsumi passed away and the old man ended up losing the farm. His luck wasn't so good."

"How did you know him?"

"He worked for me a couple years before the war started—he and Sogoji lived in a little house back by the crick. It's closed up now."

I recalled my dad mentioning that Mr. Lanski had "Japanese help" at one time. It was worth a mention because Mr. Lanski almost never hired help—except the maid, of course. The whole thing sounded fishy.

"What happened to the old man?" I demanded.

"I don't care for that tone of voice, young lady. You got a question, you ask it nice."

I swallowed, and asked in a voice that sounded nice to me, "What happened to—to this—to his dad? Sir."

"He died," Mr. Lanski said shortly. "In the spring of '42. So Sogoji's an orphan. Does that satisfy you?"

Hardly, I thought. Not looking at the Jap, I asked the most obvious question of all: "How come he's not at camp?"

"Because he didn't have any ties among the Japanese; his folks were always kind of isolated from the rest. He wanted to stay with us, so . . . we let him."

"How? I mean, how did you get away with that, sir?"

"By pretending there was no such person. See?"

I felt my mouth set in a thin, hard line. It must have taken a lot of hiding, sneaking, and outright lying to keep a secret like this. Mr. Lanski hurried on to say, "Look, little g—look, Hazel: you have a family and friends and a place to belong. What if you didn't? You'd be sad and scared, just like Sogoji."

The minute I looked at the Jap, he put on a shy, anxious smile. Sad and scared, my foot. I wasn't sure I bought any of it—even if his parents had died, how could no one else know about him? Turning back to Mr. Lanski, I demanded, "What would Jed think about this?"

The man's eyes widened in surprise. "Jed? Why, he's the one who talked us into letting Sogoji stay."

I bit my lip, feeling dumb. Of course Jed knew. And nobody in their right mind could suspect him of anything sneaky or underhanded. But that didn't mean that a certain foreigner within earshot couldn't be sneaky and underhanded. Maybe the Jap had them all fooled.

I reached into my knapsack and pulled the strip of paper from the language book, holding it out to Mr. Lanski. "Can he explain *this?*" I heard a gasp from the "secret." Got you now! I thought.

Mr. Lanski stood up, reached over, and pulled the message from my hand. After studying it a minute he sighed and shook his head. "I *told* you to be more careful with these, Sogoji."

I looked from one face to the other; the Jap dropped his eyes and twisted his hands together in a fidgety way.

Mr. Lanski turned to me. "Did you find it tangled in a bush?"

Surprised, I nodded.

"Thought so. Do you have time to pay us a visit, Hazel?"

Any spy knows you should never, never let yourself get boxed in. So I thought twice about accepting the invitation. Not that I suspected Mr. Lanski of being an actual traitor anymore, but he *could* have been duped by the enemy. And whenever Terry Lee was captured and taken to an enemy camp, he always picked up some vital piece of information for the Allies by keeping his head clear and his eyes open.

So, with all senses on alert, I followed Mr. Lanski while the Jap trailed behind us with that hatchet. I kept my back straight and my shoulders level in spite of the tingling in my spine. Don't panic, boys—stick together and follow my lead!

In all my life, I had never been inside our neighbors' house. There always seemed to be an invisible fence around it, built partly by Mrs. Lanski's "condition." The mister and missus were an odd pair, for sure. My dad used to wonder how horse-radish and cotton candy could have produced a nice, normal fellow like Jed, but every family had its ways. After that afternoon I had to agree—every family had its ways, and every house was its own little world of peculiar smells and sounds. The Lanski house smelled bland and sweet like tapioca pudding and sounded like swing band music. As we entered, a high raspy voice came from the back of the house: "Where've you all been? My shoulder is *killing* me!"

"'Scuse me a minute," Mr. Lanski muttered, and then he was gone.

That left me alone with the . . . I didn't know what to call him. The saboteur? The spy? I turned my head and found that shy, nervous smile on his face again. Standing this close to him, with no one else around, my fingers and toes turned to ice.

In newspaper and movie cartoons, Japs had wide, evil grins.

The summer after the war started, Frank made a garden scarecrow that was supposed to look like Emperor Hirohito, right down to the wax buckteeth and thick glasses made from the bottoms of Coke bottles. Mary Frances and I used to throw rocks at it, playing Air Raid on Tokyo.

Of course, a real flesh-and-blood Jap wouldn't look much like our scarecrow. But those puffy-lidded eyes and flat nose were even scarier for being real. I tried not to show any fear but stared at him stony-faced until the smile faded. Don't suck up to me, I thought. You might have fooled the Lanskis, but you won't pull the wool over these baby blues. It was a relief when he looked away and I could case the room.

It was an old-fashioned parlor, neat and cold as a museum, with a sofa and armchair covered in lace doilies, a big cabinet radio, and a fireplace with an oak mantel. Right in the middle of the mantel shelf stood a framed photo of Jed in his marine uniform. In the window hung a banner with a blue star to show that the family had a boy in the service. But not that they had a Jap in the woodshed! I jumped when Mr. Lanski stuck his head through the door and said, "Come on back."

It looked like most of the living in the Lanski house went on in the bedroom. A pan of water steamed on the flat top of the Franklin stove, a portable radio blared from the window, two canaries chirped in a wire cage, and Mrs. Lanski reigned like a queen from an armchair throne near the stove. She was talking a mile a minute, even before I was all the way in the room: "It's the little Anderson girl! I'm so happy you dropped by, dear; your sweet sister Estelle has told us so much about you, I feel like you're one of the family. Come a little closer and let me get a good look at you."

I felt like a bug when it lands in a spiderweb and the threads tremble with the approach of something big and leggy. But this was only poor Mrs. Lanski—big enough, but not leggy, and surely not dangerous. This close, she reminded me of a movie starlet who'd been blown up like a balloon. Her hair fell in limp blond curls, held back by a blue ribbon tied in a bow. She was wrapped in a bathrobe with her feet stuffed into fuzzy slippers—even though no self-respecting farm wife I knew would be caught dead in her bathrobe after six in the morning. Every breath she took ended in a little gasp. "John, honey, put some water on for tea, would you? Sogoji, my shoulder's all tight, so if you don't mind . . ." She leaned forward a little as the Jap stepped quickly around to the side of her chair and started rubbing her shoulder, his hands moving so fast they seemed to flash. Mrs. Lanski talked on, hardly pausing for a reply. "Hazel, you are the spit 'n' image of your father. What a cutup Howard was! That man could dance all night and pick apples all the next day. Of course, he was a regular tortoise compared to your mother. We used to say Marjorie was a ball of fire, just a ball of—ouch! Easy there, Sogoji!"

He was working her shoulder like my ball-of-fire mother kneaded bread dough. At the "ouch!" he bumped the tea table beside her chair and a stack of movie magazines slid off. Then he grinned and bobbed his head as though he could no more stop than a windup toy.

My brain felt numb. Between Mrs. Lanski chattering, and the Jap grinning, and horse-faced Mr. Lanski forcing a smile as he popped in to say the water was ready, I could only nod when the missus said, "Now you'll stay for tea with us, won't you, honey?"

The sun was dipping behind the hills when Mr. Lanski walked me toward home. He paused at the band of untended forest that separated our orchard from his farm. In the orangey light I noticed that his eyes, pale against his farmer's tan, were the same greenish color as Jed's. "Lookit, Hazel, you seem like a smart little—you seem like a levelheaded girl. We're in a sticky situation here; you'd be doing us a big favor to keep it to yourself. Jed would say the same."

"Why?" Usually I would be more polite, but my balance was off.

"Because . . . First off, you know how much he likes kids. He kinda took Sogoji under his wing when the boy's dad died. Felt sorry for him. We all did." That stung a little: could it be that Jed thought more of a Japanese orphan than he did of me?

"And you probably know," Mr. Lanski went on, "that we didn't want Jed to go to war. He didn't have to, either: selective service gave him a deferment to work on the farm. But he wanted to go, and the only way we can get by without him is if Sogoji's around to help."

"You could hire some of the Mexicans to help," I pointed out.

"Well, I've managed all these years without strangers, and I don't mean to start now. Lanskis take care of themselves."

Especially, I thought, when Lanskis have something to hide. "So what about that message I found? Sir."

"Oh, that." He reached into his shirt pocket and pulled out the slip of paper that I'd worked so hard at translating. "It's some kind of prayer. Sogoji copies 'em every year on his mother's birthday—good wishes to her, wherever she is. This one must've blown away. Tell you what," he offered, "you keep this. If it was dangerous I'd tear it up, right?"

I took the paper, though there didn't seem to be much point in it now.

"Mum's the word," Mr. Lanski said, and tried to smile again. "Okay?"

7

TO SAVE THE NATION

I ran most of the way home, feeling like I'd just got off the Tilt-A-Whirl at the county fair. All through the tea party, Mrs. Lanski had praised their "maid" to the skies. Why, they just didn't know how they'd get along without Sogoji. She made him sit down with us, and though I never looked at him I could feel him slurping up our conversation, meanwhile sending nervous glances my way. They were all working on me, I knew that—trying to make sure I'd keep my mouth shut. What made it so squirmy was knowing how afraid they were. Afraid of me! It was fun to imagine myself holding a squad of

Japanese prisoners in terror, but the real thing felt a little different.

"Where have you *been*?" Mom demanded when I came in through the kitchen door. "I was about ready to send Estelle out looking for you." She looked like she was about ready to spit, too, but when I explained, her anger turned to amazement. "Having tea with the *Lanskis*? Well, I never. You mean sourpuss John actually *invited* you?"

"I . . . helped him clear some brush." That was stretching the truth a little, but I owed it to Jed to keep the secret—at least for now.

"Oh. Well, that was neighborly of you. He could use some help now that he has the whole farm to care for, plus—" She broke off, but I could sense a comment about Mrs. Lanski floating in the air—if anything that big could float. "Never mind. Wash up and set the table right now. Did you forget we were having company for dinner?"

Oops—with everything else going on, I'd forgotten she had invited Mr. Mayhew. When I passed through the living room, there he was, sitting on the couch with Estelle while the radio played a Glenn Miller tune. "Hi, Hazel."

"Did I hear you got invited to the Lanskis'?" Estelle asked. "I've only been there twice. I've talked to Jed's mother a total of three times. What did you think of her?"

I shrugged. "She was nice. She gave me shortbread cookies."

"Did you see the maid?"

Warning bells went off. "A little."

"I never have. When I went over for dinner, they never let her out of the kitchen."

"That's funny," Mr. Mayhew said, like he wanted back into the conversation.

"Isn't it? When I asked, Jed said she couldn't speak much English, and it made her self-conscious."

I beat a retreat to the bathroom while Estelle was telling Mr. Mayhew about our neighbors. Over the splash of water in the sink, I heard Jed's name mentioned at least twice.

The company rated a beef roast, mashed potatoes, green beans, and sliced tomatoes in vinegar. "Eat up, Mr. Mayhew," Estelle said as she passed the meat. "You're looking at a whole month of ration points on this table."

"Please," he said. "Call me Artie."

Mom passed the potatoes. "Don't mind Estelle. She's just having a little fun. We try to do our part around here."

"That means wearing victory hand-me-downs and hitching victory rides and eating victory stew every other night of the week."

Mr. Mayhew laughed. "That's the spirit, Miss Anderson."

"Please. Call me Estelle."

"So, Hazel," Mom broke in. "Tell us about your visit."

This was tricky, talking about the Lanskis' house and Mrs. Lanski's health problems and their mystery maid without saying too much. After a few minutes, Estelle saved the day by mentioning that Jed was on his way to the Pacific. "Of course we don't know where he's going, but the rumor is jungle training on Guadalcanal."

"Oh," Mr. Mayhew said.

"Did you—I mean, do I understand that you . . . um, served there?" Estelle turned shy all of a sudden.

"Yes." Mr. Mayhew swallowed a bite of mashed potatoes, while everyone waited for more. But he didn't say any more.

"He took a piece of shrapnel in his leg," I finally explained, being helpful. Mom gave me a peeved look.

"That's right," the teacher said. "This is really a delicious dinner, Mrs. Anderson—I don't remember when I ate so well."

I figured he was eating well all over the valley, since the ladies had been lining up with dinner invitations. But my mother took the hint and changed the subject. "Tell us about your family."

It turned out that his mother had passed away and his father was in Mexico working on some government project. So he was practically an orphan, on top of his bad memories from Guadalcanal. By the time he was ready to go back to the Hedgecocks', we'd almost smothered him in sympathy. Mom turned on the outside light and all three of us followed him onto the porch. "I hate to ask," she said, "but the school board was wondering if you're getting your pension checks from the army yet."

"No, but it's nothing to worry about." Mr. Mayhew pulled

on his jacket and took an overseas cap out of the pocket. "The usual snafu."

"The what?"

"You know—'situation normal, all . . . fouled up.'" Estelle laughed, and he smiled the brightest smile I'd ever seen on his face. "Say, could somebody walk me to the road and point me in the right direction?"

He said "somebody," but he was looking right at Estelle. She hesitated, then nodded, and they stepped off the porch together. I saw my mother's eyebrows go up.

Was Sogoji dangerous? He was just a kid. Besides, the Lanskis worked him like a slave—they hardly left him any time for spying.

On the other hand, Japs were sneaky—everybody knew that. Why wouldn't he want to go away with his own people? Suppose he stayed behind so he'd be in a strategic position to send intelligence to the Japanese fleet? All he would need was a shortwave radio stowed away somewhere.

On the other hand, what could a farm boy know that was worth passing on to Admiral Yamamoto? And Jed thought Sogoji was okay. . . .

But in Sunday's episode of "Terry and the Pirates," the enemy sailor who had seemed so harmless turned out to be a spy! He'd been signaling his buddies in the area with a radio device that looked like an ordinary comb, and they had kidnapped Chan Sung! Terry was in a real fix. So was I, if the Jap next door was more than he seemed.

By Monday morning I'd thought in the same circle so many times my brain felt like a racetrack. At school, Gladys had to ask me twice about a reception that our mothers were planning for Mr. Mayhew—plus I missed half the eights in the times tables, and I couldn't even get to the second step of a long division problem.

But when Mr. Mayhew started on *Treasure Island* after recess, he got my full attention. The story was building up to a big climax: Jim Hawkins trapped on the *Hispaniola* without a friend while Israel Hand the pirate hunted him down like a dog. Jim climbed the rigging to the crow's nest, but Hand spotted him, and darned if he didn't come after Jim with a knife clenched in his teeth. Closer and closer crept the pirate as I inched up to the edge of my chair and my palms got sweaty. In my mind, Israel Hand's ugly, bearded face started to look like a smooth Japanese mug with burning black eyes and big yellow teeth. At the most exciting part, Mr. Mayhew stood up and paced, rolling on his bad leg. When it seemed that Jim was done for, the teacher pulled an imaginary pistol and shouted, "'Not another step, Mr. Hand! Not another step, or I'll blow your brains out!'"

All of a sudden everyone turned around to stare at me. Owen snickered, "Something bite you, Hazel?" I didn't realize I'd yelped out loud.

Mr. Mayhew lowered his book. "Are you all right?" he asked.

I just nodded, my face burning. Some of the girls tittered, a scratchy sound that ran over my nerves like tiny claws. Mr. Mayhew picked up the reading again and my outburst was forgotten. But I couldn't forget what scared it out of me: a picture of myself, cornered and alone while the enemy closed in. "Not another step, Sogoji . . . !"

After that, I couldn't even concentrate on Jim Hawkins's problems.

Mr. Mayhew dismissed school when the reading was over, but as everybody rushed for the door, he called, "Hazel—could you stay for a minute?"

Ivy and Gladys went green with envy and Jackie Erickson, Owen's little brother, jostled my elbow: "Hazel's in trub-ble." Ignoring all of them, I slumped over to the teacher's desk, feeling honored and flustered at the same time.

"You seem preoccupied today," he said, and his strong black eyebrows nudged together in a frown, like Terry Lee's did when he was worried. "Do you feel well?"

"Yes, sir."

"No headaches or stomachache or . . . anything?"

He appeared to be really concerned. Suddenly I thought, Here's a friend. Here's a responsible grown-up I can talk to, and he knows something about Japs already since he's tangled with them. Maybe he knew how to tell good ones from bad—if there were any good ones. "No, sir, I'm not sick." I took a quick breath. "But—"

"That's good." He took a sealed envelope out of his desk drawer. "I wondered if you could deliver this note to your mother for me."

His handwriting, neat and round as a copybook sample, spelled out *Mrs. Marjorie Anderson* on the envelope. Automatically I reached out and took it. "Sure."

"Thanks," he said.

I opened my mouth, but the words that were right there, waiting to come out, backed up on me.

"That's all, Hazel. I hope you feel better soon."

"Oh . . . thanks." I turned away, wondering why I couldn't just open up and spill the beans.

Those beans were on the boil, swelling so much inside that I might even have told my mother that night if the dinner table talk hadn't been taken up with Mr. Mayhew's stubbornness. In his note, he had turned down the school board's offer to host a reception in his honor. He wasn't comfortable with any fuss being made over his military service.

Mom's opinion was that however horrible his experience in the Pacific had been, it didn't do any good to brood.

"Who says he's brooding?" Estelle asked. "Maybe he just doesn't like a bunch of old busybodies fawning over him."

"It's not just this occasion," Mom said. "Betty Hedgecock says he hardly ever leaves his room. He should get out and meet people—take his mind off the past. Maybe even meet a nice girl."

"I say leave it alone." Estelle was picking at her food. She was in one of her rare bad moods; since Jed shipped out, we'd heard nothing from him. "If he's happy in his own little room, let him stay. He'll come out when he feels like it."

"Well, you can't sit around waiting to 'feel like it' before you do what needs to be done. . . ."

Mom used this argument for everything from dusting the house to eating your Brussels sprouts, but I wasn't listening anymore. His own little room? Sogoji had his own little house, didn't he? Not to live in; I remembered Mr. Lanski saying the house was closed up. But he'd also mentioned it was down by the "crick," and I had a pretty good idea how to find it in an afternoon. If Sogoji was up to no good, that's where the evidence would be. He couldn't keep the shortwave radio or codebooks or gunpowder right under the Lanskis' noses, could he?

So here was my solution. I'd investigate and discover once and for all if there was anything about our Jap neighbor the president needed to know. It was my duty.

8

THE HOUSE OF MITSUMI

I slept much better than the night before and could hardly sit still during school the next day. Luckily Mr. Mayhew finished reading *Treasure Island* and dismissed the class even earlier than usual.

We knew he had fixed up the woodshed in back of the school building and moved in a cot so he could spend his after-school hours taking long naps. But it was our secret. Nobody was going to tell on him because he needed the rest—he might still be suffering from beriberi or some other jungle disease. And besides, we all had better things to do than sit in a stuffy schoolhouse all afternoon. If they didn't have chores at home, the boys went trapping or fishing, while Margie, Ivy, Gladys, and sometimes Petilia went to the Thompsons' house to play records. That day, I was off like a shot as soon as Mr. Mayhew said, "Class dismissed," and stopped at home only long enough to ditch my books and change out of my dress.

Mom was at a committee meeting and Uncle Chet wouldn't be expecting me for another hour and a half. That might be just enough time.

My plan was to strike out across Anderson property until I came to the creek, then follow it upstream looking for signs of habitation. The first part was easy; the second wasn't.

There was no path running along the creek, and more than once the tangled brush and fallen trees forced me into the water. I took off my shoes and socks and rolled up the legs of my overalls, feeling for sharp rocks. Except for the chatter of the creek, the woods were hushed and still as though waiting for something to happen. I scrambled over a grassy spit where the current made a sharp bend. I should have brought a hatchet along to clear a path—Terry Lee would have had his machete and a couple of Filipino natives. But I'd just have to go it alone, like a solitary scout on some remote Pacific island—such as the island where Jed and his marine company were headed. I'd watch out for booby traps and poisonous snakes . . . and spike pits . . . and enemy soldiers. Whatever happened, I couldn't be surprised.

Then I was surprised. A forest of bamboo speared up right in front of me, the stalks leaning so far over they blocked my way. Bamboo in Oregon? Just beyond it, the water spilled into a deep pool. It looked impossible to go any farther, until I spotted the ghost of a path opening up on the left. Through the vines and pines and hemlock trees I could barely make out the mossy roof of a house. Objective in view!

Little whips of brush and vine smacked my arms and face, but I kept pushing up the path until it opened into a clearing. There stood the house: just a shack made of sawn boards with a porch in front and an outhouse behind. The ground all around it was cleared, even though creeper vines were crawling up to the stone foundation.

Nothing about it looked Japanese. I was half expecting one of those paper houses with sliding doors, but this could have been any abandoned homestead in the good old U.S.A., even to the boarded-up windows and the planks crossed over the front door. I slipped across the yard and crept up the porch steps, keeping to the far edges so they wouldn't squeak. NO TRES-PASSING was painted on one of the boards over the door. My parents taught me to respect signs like that, but any law officer knows that there are times to break the rules. Besides—the door was open a crack, a sight that made me catch my breath and freeze.

No doubt about it: the cleared yard and the open door proved that somebody was still using this house. Maybe even right now. I stood still as a fence post, listening so hard there was nothing to me but ears. At the sound of a rustle from inside, I almost jumped off the porch. But on second thought, the sound was too small to be anything but a mouse. And would mice feel free to scurry if there was anything bigger to scare them away?

Good thinking. And now I'd better move fast. The door creaked when I pushed it just far enough to let me duck under the boards and slip through.

Then I stood blinking in a pale slab of light. It looked like a parlor-kitchen-dining room, with an iron cookstove and a table at one end and an open door leading to the bedroom on the other. No wires, cartridges, or vacuum tubes; nothing on the walls but pegs for hanging clothes and dark patches where pictures used to be. If there was anything to hide, I couldn't see a place to hide it. The oven door stood wide open, as if to say "Don't shoot—I'm innocent!" The twigs of a bird's nest poked from the oven, but even the birds had deserted. I crossed the room slowly, pausing at every squeak in the floorboards, until I stood on the threshold of the bedroom door.

Here at last was something worth discovering.

On the north window, one of the lower boards had been knocked out to let in light. Just below it stood a tall, narrow table spread with a white cloth. On the table was a squarish object I couldn't make out from that distance. I tiptoed close enough to recognize a small wooden crate turned on its side, the open end covered with a lace curtain. In front of the opening were two candles in brass candlesticks. Something made me hesitate—a thought that I might be trespassing on more than just property—but curiosity won out. And duty, of course. With my heart beating so loud I could have marched to it, I lifted the curtain and laid it back on the top of the box.

Whatever I'd expected, it wasn't this. Two photographs were propped up on opposite sides of the box, with a plain china dish between them and some kind of card leaning against the back. The card was made from layers of colored paper with one sheet of shiny gold folded in. The colors framed a picture of a mountain, with Japanese characters down one side. It was too fancy to be a secret message. Secret messages had to be simple and small so you could stick them in your shoe or swallow them if you got caught. I reached in carefully and picked up one of the photographs.

The man in it was wearing a checkered suit with a high starched collar, the kind of outfit my grandfather Anderson used to wear. He was small, with bags under his slanted eyes, a skimpy mustache, and a very serious expression. He wore a bowler hat and carried a book in one arm, like a teacher on his way to class. If it was Sogoji's father, he looked like a Japanese diplomat or professor or something. But Mr. Lanski had said he was only a busted farmer. The imprint in the corner read *Clymer Studios, Portland, Oregon.*

The other photo had Japanese characters stamped in the

corner and showed a lady in a kimono. She stood beside an armchair in what looked like an American parlor—probably the photography studio. Her hands held a chrysanthemum and her eyes looked down and off to the side as though they were too shy to meet the camera. Her face, under the piled-up black hair, was sweet without being pretty. She wore an anxious little smile that seemed eager to please—but afraid that it wouldn't. With a start, I remembered seeing that smile on Sogoji's face.

Very carefully, I put the pictures back and lowered the curtain over them. My face felt hot, as though I'd found out more than I wanted to know. Thoughts of the little family that used to live here flitted across my mind like paper scraps across an empty floor, making me feel sad and sorry.

But sorry for what, exactly, I couldn't say.

Mr. Mayhew didn't have another book lined up to read after *Treasure Island,* so we went back to times table drills and state capitals for an afternoon. But on Friday, Gladys brought her copy of *Five Little Peppers and How They Grew* to school, and for an hour after lunch the teacher plowed through the adventures of Ben, Polly, Davie, Joel, and little Phronsie Pepper as they struggled to help their poor widowed mother keep food on the table. Half the student body was snoozing away at their desks when he snapped the book shut and announced, "Class dismissed." The last we saw of him, he was headed for the woodshed.

Sherman was beginning to complain about early dismissals. "*Now* what do we do? I can't tell my mom I'm collecting scrap paper again. She barely believed me last time."

"Dry up," Roger told him. "He's the best teacher we ever had."

"He's not a teacher at all! I haven't learned anything since this term started."

The other boys groaned. "So go to the library," Marvin snarled. "It's Friday—you've got all weekend to learn something, *Sherman.*"

"Sherman the German," Owen and Roger chimed in, while Sherman turned red all the way to the tips of his ears. His last name being Schultz, he was bound to get stuck with this nickname. But if he were big and strong like Marvin or smart enough to laugh, it wouldn't have stuck for long. Instead, Sherman always blew up and protested that his family bought more war bonds than anybody in the valley and his brother reported war news for the local paper and where would we be without war bonds or news? He used to get into fights with Owen before Owen got a whole lot bigger all of a sudden.

Now he just sputtered, which only made the boys laugh until Marvin said, "Aw, this is stupid. I'm gonna check my rabbit traps." That broke everybody up—the boys, anyway. The girls had already started down the road toward the Thompson house, and for the first time I wished they would ask me to go along. Since it looked like Sogoji was just a harmless little or-

phan after all (even though he happened to be Japanese), all the
fun had gone out of scouting around Hawk's Nest. Not even
"Terry and the Pirates" interested me much that week.

Just as well, probably, because Uncle Chet needed me in the
orchard every spare minute. That Friday afternoon I tried to
convince myself that picking apples was just as important to the
war effort as catching enemy spies, but it was hard going.

Estelle and I spent all Saturday morning in the packing
shed, where the apples had piled up so high that Mom was re-
cruited to help. After we walked home and I was grilling cheese
sandwiches for lunch, Estelle got a call from an old boyfriend. I
heard her tell him that she wasn't interested in going out, but
still the conversation went on a little too long, it seemed to me.
After we all sat down and tucked into our soup and sandwiches,
I muttered, "Some engagement you've got going."

"What's that supposed to mean?" Estelle demanded.

Mom set down her spoon, lining it up with the edge of the
place mat. "I think Hazel means that it's unbecoming to flirt
with other boys when you claim to be serious about Jed."

"Flirt?! Joe and I were just laughing over old times."

"It sounded to me like you were leaving it open for him to
call back, which just proves what I've told you. You're not ready
to tie yourself down—"

"I don't need my family to monitor my phone
conversations—"

"Watch that tone of voice, *young lady*—"

Next minute they were both yelling, which never used to happen when Daddy was at home. He had a low, quiet way of saying things that evened out the balance when feelings tipped too far one way or another. I gobbled my sandwich, slurped up my soup, and excused myself, with Mom hardly noticing. Then I grabbed my air patrol gear and beat it.

On my way up the hill I felt for Jed's silver dollar in my pocket and wondered if he'd reached his destination yet: Guadalcanal, if Estelle was right. Jungle training. I took a detour off the path, crouching low and slipping through the brush unseen by any spy planes that happened to be on patrol. After the marines landed on the island, I'd reveal myself to Jed. He'd be mad, of course, but once he found out what I could do, he'd secretly thank his lucky stars. I was small, and I didn't eat much, and I could move as quick and silent as a snake. After a week or two, if I happened to mention Estelle, he'd say, "Estelle who?"

When I finally reached Hawk's Nest, a little scratched, I swept the field glasses in a circle for a quick survey—wishing, for the thousandth time, for a real observation tower. Then I centered the lenses on Mount Hood. Breathing slow and steady, the way Frank taught me, I started turning five minutes clockwise with each breath. It was a way to keep from rushing when I felt rushed, but now I was using it to help me concentrate on planes instead of my sister. From Mount Hood the field glasses ticked west, then north, and on toward the east.

And there, with my field glasses trained on the Lanskis'

backyard, I nearly croaked. Another pair of lenses was aimed up from the near side of their garden, looking right at *me.*

Even my thoughts froze for a minute. The other field glasses dropped, and there was Sogoji behind them, the yellow sunbonnet pushed back. He was spying on me!

Then he grinned, drew himself up, and made a broad salute, the flat of his hand bouncing off his forehead.

He was making fun of me, that's what. It was like being called Sherman the German, only worse. He made me feel like the hours and hours I'd spent on this hill all by myself were nothing but a game.

Well, Mr. Jap, I thought, I haven't made up my mind about you yet, but you can bet my eye's on you until I do. And in the meantime, you are *not* going to keep me from my patriotic duty.

I didn't wave back, needless to say. When I finally finished my surveillance and checked the Lanskis' yard again, he wasn't there anymore.

9

WHAT TO DO ABOUT "CHARLIE"

Mr. Mayhew kept plugging away at *Five Little Peppers* and finished it in only four afternoons, reading fast and (I think) skipping the boring parts. Gladys was ready for him and brought a copy of *Mrs. Wiggs and the Cabbage Patch* before he could start on times tables again. I promised myself that before he got to the end of that one, I'd have some literature on hand that was more exciting.

Even Mrs. Wiggs was some relief from picking apples. The harvest season was winding down, but since two of our workers had left, Uncle Chet was making do, and he wasn't too happy about making do with an eleven-year-old girl (even though I was almost twelve). I felt like I was drowning in apples and came up for air only once that week.

That was on Wednesday. Estelle got off work early to help out in the packing shed, and when I got home from school, she ran up and waved a letter under my nose. "It's from Jed!"

All I saw at first was a stack of heavy black bars lying among the scribbles. "Why did he cross out so much?"

"That's the censor, knucklehead. All letters are censored so no important information gets out to the enemy. We don't even know for sure where he is."

"So what good is the letter?" I was feeling a little put out that she got to it before I did.

"It says he's alive! He's been promoted to Pfc! And he loves me to pieces. Look." She pointed to the bottom of the second page, where Jed had written, *Be good, and remember that I love you to pieces.*

"I see it." I was thinking he might have spared a "piece" for me when Estelle added, "Oh, I almost forgot. He put in a note for you."

She reached for the lamp table, but I'd already spotted the square of folded paper and pounced before Estelle did. Then I escaped to the bedroom, where I plopped on my bed and read the note in one long gulp. On the surface it seemed perfectly ordinary. But I could read between the lines:

Hi, Hazel, I can't tell you where I am, but it's hotter and steamier than a Chinese laundry. You should see me [this part was blocked out by the censor], *it's like picking strawberries all day only not so much fun, ha ha. My dad wrote me that you had a run-in with Charlie. Some pup, huh? But he's a good dog. May look a little scary, but he won't bite. I'm glad you found him, he could use a friend.*

Have you still got my silver dollar?

So long, pardner—

After I'd read the note enough times to have it memorized, I just sat on the bed getting more confused. It was nice to think he trusted me enough to be glad I'd found "Charlie," and it was fun to share a secret with him that Estelle didn't know. Still— Sogoji might not bite, but it was hard to forget that the first time I'd seen him, he chased me with a hatchet. Who needed "friends" like that?

Still, I would climb Mount Hood backward on my knees for Jed if he really really wanted me to. So how much did he want me to be friends with Sogoji?

I was worrying so hard I barely noticed that Mr. Mayhew let us out extra early on Friday, but Mom did. *"Good,"* she said when I showed up. "I was picking until two and now I'm way behind with housework. I need you to sweep every room while I take out the rugs, and then you can fill up the water jugs to haul over to the orchard. It's been so warm today they'll need it."

I'll say it was warm—by the time I hauled two gallons of

water all the way to the orchard, I was sweating. Uncle Chet was behind schedule: the Newton apples had started to ripen as the Gravensteins were playing out, and a whole crop of Red Delicious had come in earlier than he expected. The minute I showed up, he said, "I need you to pick the low branches along this row, Hazel. The fellows left 'em for you. I may need you all day Monday, too—this is exactly why I told your dad not to let Frank go. . . ."

He'd told everybody this, lots of times. Daddy thought the Young America Corps would be good for Frank—toughen him up and teach him some skills that Daddy wasn't around to teach. Daddy was usually right, in my opinion—but with apples falling all over the orchard, it didn't make sense that a perfectly good pair of hands was down in Gresham helping build an armory for strangers.

I missed Frank's brain a lot more than his apple-picking hands, though. Frank had been friends with Japs before—he could give me the lowdown if anybody could. I was trying to figure out how to write a letter that would explain the situation but not give much away if it fell into the wrong hands—

"Hazel!" Uncle Chet yelled at me. "Where's your head? I've been calling you—come over here!"

"Gas tank's low," he said when I dashed over. "Can's in the packing shed. Two gallons. Hurry." The more behind he got, the more words dropped out of his conversation, but I understood he wanted me to fetch a two-gallon can of gasoline. The packing shed wasn't too far away, but it was downhill, meaning that after finding the can, I had to drag it uphill. I was huffing like a locomotive when I got back to the pickers. Uncle Chet looked away from his tree just long enough to say, "Go ahead and pour it in. Then take the tractor down to the south end with Miguel and Anthony and start loading."

I took a crate from the trailer and turned it over to give myself some height over the gas tank. The tractor growled at me as fumes from the fuel tank shivered the air. I was wondering if Frank remembered any of the codes in his Boy Scout book. If so, I could write him a letter in code. But I'd have to keep it short so he would have time to decipher it. And I'd have to find some way to tell him it wasn't just a game and maybe avoid using the word *Japanese* but find a word that he would understand to mean *Japanese*—

"HAZEL! For God's sake, stop!"

Uncle Chet's voice sizzled. Then I looked down and saw the motor block was on fire from the gasoline I'd spilled on it.

I jumped off the crate—spilling more gasoline. A little cloud of flame exploded in my face. Uncle Chet elbowed me to one side as he stripped off his jacket and beat the motor block with it. Two field hands rushed in and stomped on the puddles of blazing gasoline. It was all over in less than a minute.

My hair smelled funny. I reached up and felt the crinkly tips of my bangs breaking off. Uncle Chet cut the engine and looked it over, discovering that the insulation had been burned off some of the wires. He'd have to go back to the machine shed and get more wire to replace them.

After cussing out the tractor, he started in on me. He watched his language because I was a girl, but according to him I was a lot of other things besides, like an airy-fairy dreamer who couldn't be trusted with responsibility: "Don't you know enough to cut the engine *before* you start putting gas in? If you can't do a simple job without setting the orchard on fire, what good are you?"

I couldn't think of an answer. Instead I turned around and took off running.

I felt like a balloon blown up tight enough to pop. All the pressure that had been building up for three weeks, since Jed left and I found the note and discovered its secret and worried over what to do about it—all that propelled me the whole way to the observation hill. At the bottom of the slope the pains in my side made me slow down to a walk, but I kept going, though I didn't know why.

The sun was low by then: just a red sliver showed, looking over its shoulder at the day it was leaving behind. A breeze dried the sweat on my face and raised goose bumps on my arms. Pretty soon the winter chill would move in and hunker down, and the apple trees would rattle their branches in the north wind like rows of skeletons.

I was blubbering like a baby, my eyes so misty the whole landscape was swimming. It wasn't fair, what Uncle Chet said—

I'd filled dozens of gas tanks without mishap, and a few little drips didn't amount to a whole orchard going up in smoke. Daddy wouldn't have yelled at me like that, would he? I wasn't an airy-fairy dreamer. Was I? I walked right past the flag and over to the far side of Hawk's Nest, where the hill sloped down into Lanski property. There I wiped my eyes on my sleeve, and my nose, too.

The kitchen window of the Lanskis' house threw a little pool of light on the ground, crossed by the shadow of somebody moving around inside. I wiped my eyes again and squinted at the window. Though it was too far away to make out any details, Sogoji had to be the one in the kitchen. Mr. Lanski was too tall and the missus too wide. And both of them moved slower than the dark little figure flitting in and out of sight. I stared at him for a while, sniffling. I still didn't know for sure whether he was dangerous or not, whether the Lanskis were dupes or worse, whether I'd done anything right since finding that little slip of paper.

But one thing was sure: I didn't want to make my way home in the dark. I turned around, noticing the flagpole. Something didn't look right about it. A wad of stuff, pale and squishy-looking as a fungus, was bunched up just below the flag.

Coming closer, I reached out and squeezed it, feeling a rubbery give to the material. A couple of long tails hung down from the knot. Even though I hadn't seen anything like them for a while, I knew right away what they were: nylon stockings. When I untied them from the pole, a piece of paper fell out.

Just enough light was left to make out the words, printed in block letters: TO HAZL. FOR WAR EFORT.

"What in the world!" I said out loud, sounding like my mother. Sogoji? He must have got these from Mrs. Lanski. But did she give them up voluntarily, or was this all his idea?

I looked back at the kitchen window, staring hard. Nothing moved inside; maybe he was taking dinner on a tray to the lady of the house. But in the gathering dark, the light shone brighter and looked friendlier than it had before.

10

FRIENDLY FRITTERS

To my surprise, Mom didn't say much about the tractor: "Accidents happen. But your mind's been wandering more than usual lately—please try harder to pay attention."

She might have had a little disagreement with Uncle Chet. It happened sometimes: she'd lay into her own chicks, but if anybody else did, she could be one mad mother hen. I suspected this even more on Saturday morning when Uncle Chet apologized, sort of. "You didn't set us back too much. Besides, I should have been the one to turn off the engine before you poured the gasoline in. Want a peppermint?"

I took a peppermint and went to join Estelle in the packing shed.

Our job there was to sort all the apples picked during the last few days, cull the bruised ones, and pack the rest two layers deep in cardboard boxes—"snug enough so they won't rattle but loose enough so they won't bruise," as Aunt Ruth told us every year. The last step was to paste an *Anderson's Best* label on the side of the box and stack the boxes in the pickup for Uncle Chet to take to Hood River. My favorite part was sticking the label on. *Anderson's Best*—that was *us*. "What if we had a contest for the Best Anderson," I said to Estelle. "Who would win?"

"Huh?" She slapped a label on a box.

"Who's the Best Anderson?"

"Not me, that's for sure." She hauled the box out to the pickup.

The lift from Jed's letter didn't last more than a couple of days—lately Estelle had been acting more like a rock than a beach ball. "Are you going out with the girls tonight?" I asked when she came back in.

"No." She grabbed another box and plunked it on the packing table. "Marianne has a date and Sue and Tracy are taking the train to Portland to visit Sue's brother. Tracy's sweet on him all of a sudden. Guess I'll stay home again and do some more mending. Yippee."

"Uncle Chet would let us ride down to Hood River with

him this afternoon. We could go to a movie. *The Fighting Sullivans* is still on at the Bijou."

"That's my idea of a perfect Saturday afternoon: sitting in a stuffy theater watching war movies with a pack of screaming ten-year-olds."

My feelings must have showed, because when she glanced up and saw my face, her voice changed. "Sorry—I didn't mean you. You're sweet to ask, but I'll just stick around here this afternoon." She packed a whole layer of the box in silence, then said, "This is so hard."

"Packing apples?"

"*No.* It's hard not knowing where he is or when he'll come back or what shape he'll be in if he does. I used to think I understood how those mothers and wives and sweethearts felt, but I didn't. I don't know if I'm cut out for this."

"For what?"

"Waiting. Worrying. The time just crawls by."

It didn't seem to me she had much choice. And nobody had made her get secretly engaged. "You'll look back on this and laugh," I said, trying to sound sympathetic.

She threw a culled apple at me, but not hard. "Ha, ha. See— I'm laughing now."

If she knew what I knew, she might have been more excited. There was a Jap next door making contributions to the war effort! But I didn't know why, and I meant to find out. As soon as Uncle Chet let us off for the afternoon, I raced home and gobbled a tuna sandwich, then rushed out the door with the field glasses before Mom could give me anything else to do.

My plan was to settle this thing once and for all. After my usual area surveillance, I meant to march down the other side of the hill, knock on the Lanskis' door, and demand to speak with Sogoji. There were things I had to know: What's up with the stockings? How come you didn't want to go with the other Japanese when they were sent to camp? And is there any special reason Jed thinks you need a friend?

But after making a very thorough surveillance and a very careful report in my logbook, the whole march-down-there-and-demand-to-speak-with-Sogoji idea seemed easier said than done. I spent at least half an hour watching clouds roll in before admitting I was afraid to do it.

That was ridiculous. He was just a kid, and maybe all he was trying to do was be friendly. I stood up and clenched my fists, working up my nerve. But before I had worked up very much, a movement in the Lanskis' yard caught my attention.

Sogoji had come out to work in the garden. He moved like a hen picking its way along the rows, the yellow sunbonnet bobbing up and down, up and down as he pulled bush bean plants.

That sunbonnet made me mad—it had fooled me for almost three years. I cupped my hands into a megaphone, shouting, "HEY!"

It took a couple of yells to get his attention. When he

looked up, I was standing on the open part of the hill with my feet apart and hands on my hips. To my annoyance he did the same thing: put his feet apart and planted his hands on his hips.

I swept my right arm up in a quarter circle: come up here!

He pushed the sunbonnet back and glanced around the yard as though looking for permission. Then he held up a finger, signaling "Wait a minute," ran back to the house, and disappeared through the kitchen door. When he came out, minus the sunbonnet, he was carrying some kind of package in one hand.

With so much brush and scrub oak in the way I couldn't track his progress up the hill. I just waited, my heart pounding louder and louder, until he appeared.

For a while we stared at each other, tongue-tied. Then I burst out with, "Have you been spying on me?"

He blinked. "Spying? I thought that's what you do up here."

"I'm not spying, I'm watching."

"Then I watch you watching. What for do you watch? For planes?"

That raised my suspicions. Maybe it was just an idle question, but I didn't trust him yet. "Birds," I said firmly. Then, "Did the stockings belong to Mrs. Lanski?"

He nodded.

"Did she give them to you?"

He thought this over, then said, "She volunteered. But she don't know it."

"You mean you volunteered them for her?"

He smiled that anxious smile I'd seen on the face of the Japanese lady in the photograph in his house. But instead of admitting anything, he changed the subject. "Today I made some apple fritter. You want one?"

In his hand was a dish towel wrapped around a saucer. When he threw back one side of the towel, the smell went straight to my nose. Did I *want* one? Of course they could be poisoned . . . but no poison in the world could smell that good. My mouth was watering so much I had to swallow before saying, "Sure."

He came closer and sat cross-legged on the grass, and I did, too. The fritters were about the size of my fist, crisp on the outside and chewy on the inside, with fat nuggets of apple all the way through. The first few bites took me to heaven, and I didn't come back until it was all gone. Licking the sugar off my fingers, I noticed the other fritter was still on the plate. "Isn't that one for you?"

"Only if you don't want." He was holding himself still (except for the two fingers twiddling on his knee), trying hard to be polite. Well, I did want it, but I could be polite, too.

"No, you made 'em. You go ahead. They're really good," I added as his hand darted out quick as a bird's claw and closed on it.

"You honor me to say. Please accept my humble thanks."

"Sure, but I should be thanking you. So, uh . . . *arigato gozaimas.*"

He looked puzzled for a minute, then ducked his head with a big grin. His teeth were a little crooked, but they didn't stick out like the buckteeth in the cartoons. *"Domo, domo."*

"Did I just say thank you?"

"Yes. Me too, just shorter."

"Okay. But what about the stockings? Are you sure I should take them, since Mrs. Lanski doesn't exactly know?"

He wiped his mouth, very neat. "She won't miss. Never wears 'em. She has more, but if I take, she'll miss." He finished off the fritter and wiped his hands on the dish towel. "Allow me to ask, why does U.S. government want stockings? Who wears?"

His *a*'s and *e*'s sounded almost alike, and his *l*'s came out a little rough, like *r*'s. That surprised me, because in the comics, Orientals always say *r*'s like *l*'s. "Nobody wears them. The army makes parachute cords and things like that. They melt the nylon down somehow and make fibers that they twist into cord that won't break."

"Ah." He nodded—and kept nodding, until I felt like putting a hand on his head to stop him.

"Don't you ever hear the war news and salvage announcements on the radio?"

Now his head went the other direction. "Not in house, so much. Lula-san don't like it. She keeps music on, but when it's time for news, she turns off. Lanski-san, he listens sometimes in the shed."

"I see." This squared with what my mother said about Mrs. Lanski not wanting to admit there was a war going on. She'd have a harder time pretending that, I thought, if she had to live like most farm wives instead of like a queen. "Who taught you to cook?"

He blinked, as though taken by surprise. "My father, some. Lula-san, a little. *Better Homes and Gardens* most of all."

I remembered seeing a few copies of the magazine lying among the *True Romances* and *Silver Screens* in Mrs. Lanski's room. "So you taught yourself?"

"I must be useful."

But why? I wondered. Why did he put up with all the ordering around, and wearing a sunbonnet, and having to keep out of sight? "Why didn't you want to go with the other Japs— Japanese?" I asked him. As though embarrassed to be mentioned, he looked toward the ground with a peculiar sideways slant. Again I remembered the photo of his mother, who was holding her head in just that way when the camera clicked. "It's probably not so bad at camp," I went on. "You wouldn't have to work so much."

"Work is okay."

"But wouldn't you rather be with your friends? People your own age? Join a softball league? *Cook?*"

He kept shaking his head and looking at the ground.

Something's going on here, I thought—but he wasn't about to tell me. Instead he reached for the dish towel and folded it around the saucer, scrambling to his feet. "Must go. Happy watching."

He moved as quick and silent as a mouse—he was already to the edge of the hill before I even could stand up. "Wait!" He turned, and then I was the one who felt like glancing away. "I'm here most Saturdays and some weekday afternoons. If you want to come up again, it's okay with me."

He stared at me with his mouth open, then an all-out smile spread over his whole face. I wasn't sure about my reasons for making the invitation—friendship or Knowing the Enemy?— but when he smiled, it seemed like the right thing to do.

11

THE TEAM

Mr. Mayhew finished with *Mrs. Wiggs* early the following
week. Before Gladys could get to him with another goody-two-
shoes book, I walked up to his desk and plopped *Smilin' Jack and
the Jungle Pipeline* on it.

He stared like it might bite. "What's this?"

"One of my brother's Big Little books, sir. I thought you
could read it next."

He flipped through the pages. Big Little books were an inch
thick but only about three inches square, with the story printed
on every left page and a picture on every right. One story could

take up a whole afternoon, and Mr. Mayhew could make it at least as exciting as *Treasure Island,* owing to his personal experience. But: "I'd rather not read anything that has to do with the war, Hazel."

I wondered if Mom wasn't right about him getting on with getting over. His body was getting over just fine. The girls' baking brigade was shoveling doughnuts at him so fast he'd lost that lean, haunted look that went with his uniform—in fact, I wasn't even sure the uniform would fit now. "Maybe you'd like to look at it later?"

"No, thanks." He handed the book back to me. "I'll catch a ride to the Hood River Library this afternoon and find something to read."

When he called the class in after lunch recess and started dividing us up for math drills, I thought about giving him another chance at *Smilin' Jack.* But then Margie raised her hand. "When do we start on the Christmas program, sir?"

"Christmas program? Isn't it a little early for that?"

"It's the middle of October already. And there's a lot to do."

Mr. Mayhew put down the math textbook. "Like what?"

Everybody explained at once: "We have to learn some songs." "And a canned food collection . . ." "Please please please can I be an angel this year?" "Last year we made candles. . . ." "It's *stupid.*"

The more we explained, the less Mr. Mayhew seemed to understand, but after a while he got everyone to pipe down and said he would take suggestions for the program one at a time. Ideas started going up on the blackboard: Carols, Nativity Scene ("I've *got* to be an angel!" Susie shouted), Star-Spangled B., Read Xmas Message from Pres. Roosevelt, Candles. "No candles," protested Marvin. "They'll stink the place up like the Catholic church."

It took some time for Mr. Mayhew to restore order after that; we only have a few Catholic kids, but they're noisy. "That's enough!" he finally shouted. When everybody settled down, he continued, "Let's go back to one at a time, and wait until I call on you. Margie?"

Margie stood, straightened her plaid skirt, and waited until the room was absolutely quiet before saying, "I think we should include a salute to our veterans—especially you, sir."

Loud cheers broke out as Margie looked around, blinking with surprise. It was the most popular suggestion she had ever made. We all looked at Mr. Mayhew, who had set down his chalk and was slowly brushing the dust off his hands.

"Class, let me say this just once. What I did was no more than a lot of young guys who are buried in Guadalcanal, and I don't deserve any special recognition for it. They—a lot of guys—" He seemed to be having trouble with his voice, and we all looked down at our desks, squirming. "If you want to honor veterans, just leave me out."

A moment of silence followed, because no one could think what to say. Then Jackie Erickson spoke up. "Can we sing that new song? 'Rudolph the Red-Nosed Reindeer'?" Everybody started talking again, and finally we made some decisions.

Margie's mother, the director of the Methodist church choir, would arrange the musical parts of the program. Five students would write a play before Thanksgiving, and everybody else would work on decorations. The chief decoration would be a school tree decked out with paper chains and ornaments made from tin cans (donated to the scrap metal drive right after Christmas). We'd start saving cans and other supplies now and begin rehearsals the first week in December.

School let out when it was supposed to, for a change.

I got put on the playwriting committee, only because Gladys drafted me: "Hazel's always dreaming up stuff—she ought to be able to dream up a good story." Everybody laughed, but Mr. Mayhew took it seriously enough to write my name on the board. At dinner that night, Mom seemed to think it was a big honor, but she frowned when I told her about Mr. Mayhew's response to Margie's suggestion.

"Somebody should lay down the law to him," Mom said while laying down the butter on her bread. "If he doesn't appreciate his own contribution, he could let the rest of us appreciate it."

"Maybe he's hiding some deep dark secret," Estelle suggested.

"The other girls at school think so," I said. "They use up all their recess time gossiping about it."

"Whatever it is, he should quit running away," Mom said firmly. "Now that you've mentioned it, Hazel, I think the school board might want to order a quiet, dignified little plaque and present it to him after the program, with a note of our appreciation. . . ."

I decided it wasn't my problem if the teacher took offense at a quiet, dignified little plaque.

On Friday afternoon Margie wanted to settle a few details about the program, which led to a fight over whether to use a doll or a live baby Jesus in the Nativity scene. Petilia and Ivy both had baby relatives who would be *perfect*. "But I've got a ten-pound sack of flour that wants the part," Owen protested. "It doesn't screech like Ivy's baby nephew and it's better-looking, too."

Mr. Mayhew had his hands full settling the girls after that one. Throughout the uproar Margie sat with her lips pressed together and her arm stuck up like a flagpole.

When the teacher finally called on her, she stood up. "I think it's shameful to be *fighting* over who plays the *Prince* of *Peace*."

A few of the boys groaned, but Mr. Mayhew slapped his desk with an open hand. "Hear, hear. I'm letting school out early, and I want you all to spend the weekend thinking about what Margie said."

Nobody seemed to be thinking about what Margie said when they hit the school yard and scattered in different directions. I wasn't, for sure—I was wondering if Sogoji would join me next day on the hill.

I didn't have to wonder—meeting him turned out to be the simplest thing in the world. He was watching for me after lunch, and when the sun bounced off my field glasses into the kitchen window, he stepped outside the back door and waved. About twenty minutes later he came up with a blanket and a handful of saltine crackers—no baking that afternoon, I guess. He spread out the blanket and we sat on it cross-legged, facing each other. It startled me all over again, seeing his half-moon eyelids and sharp cheekbones right here in my special place. "So . . . ," I began. "When do you have to be back?"

He shrugged. "Lula-san sleeps a couple hour every afternoon. She says she's glad I have a playmate."

I groaned. "*Playmate.* That sounds like we're both about five years old." He shrugged again, smiling. "How old are you, anyway?"

"Fifteen, las' June."

"*What?*" This came out so fast and loud he jumped, but that's how surprised I was. I'd been thinking he was my age or even younger. He looked like a poor little match boy, with his shoes too small and his shirt and pants too big, but— "You're as old as my brother!" I leaned forward and grabbed his sleeve. "Frank Anderson—you must have been in his grade at school! Do you remember Frank?"

His eyes were darting every which way as though trying to escape. "School?" he repeated. "No, no school."

"What do you mean? Didn't you go to school?"

He found something to stare at on the ground as he gently pulled his sleeve out of my grasp. "Sometime . . . sometime back. For two year, until I was eight. Then Father took me out."

"What for?"

He shook his head. "I'm pretty dumb. Never learn to read much."

"Well, of course not, if you don't stay in school—"

"Mama died," he said, still not looking at me. "Father took me traveling, looking for work. Down to California, back up through Oregon, finally back here."

Tired of not being looked at, I leaned way over and turned my face so it was right in his line of sight. "Hello?" I waved, and his lips twitched a little. His eyes followed me when I sat up again. "What did you do all the time he was working?"

"Worked with, sometimes. When he was picking fruits down in Medford. That was okay. In the cities, it was hard. Like Sacramento. I stayed in the rooming house most days. Didn't go out much, because not many people like Japanese. Not even Chinese like Japanese."

This was the most he'd ever said at one time, and I was struggling to take it all in. "So you spent days in a rooming house with nothing to do? Nobody to talk to?"

"No. Except—" He stopped himself. "But excuse me."

"Excuse you for what?" Talking to him sometimes was like following a maze. "Except for what?"

"You will laugh."

"I won't, I promise. Cross my heart and hope to die."

He looked away again. "Okay. Except for Kintaro. The Golden Boy. My mother used to tell stories of him; all Japanese children know Kintaro."

I didn't laugh. "Tell me about him."

"Okay." His voice shifted to a higher pitch and became a little singsongy. "They say Saruta Kurando was a great warrior for the emperor but fell into disgrace and had to flee from court and his beautiful wife, Yaigori. She searched up and down for him, and when at last she found, he was living in a rough seaport town, keeping a low-down tavern. He felt so bad for her to see him like this, he took his own miserable life. She was so sad she fled into the forest and died, too, while giving birth to the son of Kurando. Before dying she named him Kintaro. Kintaro was raised by animals of the forest—he learned their talk, their ways. No human child to play with.

"But one day, when Kintaro was grown, he heard a voice cry for help, deep in the woods. He ran like a leopard to the sound and found a man drowning in a deep pool under a waterfall. Kintaro leapt, down down down into the pool, and saved the man, who it happened to be a noble kinsman of the emperor! The man looked over Kintaro and said, 'Ah, so!' because he was grown so big and strong. The noble kinsman brought him to Kyoto, where his strength like bear and courage like tiger and cunning like fox made him a mighty hero. To this day, every boy wants to be like Kintaro."

"Including you?"

He glanced down again. "I am not strong or brave or cunning."

"Well . . . you make the best apple fritters I ever ate. If the emperor got to try them, you'd be the imperial fritter fryer."

He frowned. "You mean Hirohito?"

"No, I mean Kintaro's emperor, a story emperor. It's a joke."

The frown changed to a smile—a shaky smile, like he was trying it on for size. "Good. I am a true American."

The funny thing was, I was starting to believe him.

At school the next week, Margie Holmes managed to take up a few more afternoons with program plans. First, the fight over who would play baby Jesus was settled when Mr. Mayhew decided there was no room for a Nativity scene. That meant Susie Lopez would have to go somewhere else to be an angel. She wasn't happy, but the boys whooped and hollered when they heard they wouldn't have to dress up in towels and bathrobes.

That left the coast clear for Margie and her mother to push their own ideas. Mrs. Holmes wanted to teach us a Christmas carol she'd learned when she was a girl: "Watchman, Tell Us of the Night." It was about a traveler on a night journey who comes near a city and asks the watchman if there's a mysterious star in the heavens. (Though it seemed to me that if the traveler wanted to know, he could just look up into the heavens for himself.) The play would be about a family with a son in the service—*watching* for his return, get it? On Christmas Eve they would be sitting around the radio listening to news and wishing for an end to the war so the star of peace could rise.

It didn't sound like much of a story, but the class had already shot down my ideas, like "The Hood River Christmas Eve Bombing Raid." We were sick of arguing, so the vote was almost unanimous to get stuck with—I mean, to write—a play built around "Watchman, Tell Us of the Night." We would have to learn the song anyway.

"It's not that *bad,* really," I told Sogoji on our next Saturday afternoon. "Just boring."

"If you wrote play—"

"*The* play," I corrected him.

"If you wrote *the* play, would it be boring?"

"Heck, no. It would be about the Hood River Junior Commandos. On Christmas Eve they're listening to their shortwave radio and happen to pick up a signal that's so low none of the government receivers catch it, and because they've been studying Japanese, they make out enough to know it's a plan to bomb the shipyards in Seattle! But nobody believes them until they spot an enemy reconnaissance plane and convince army intelligence to track it down. So on Christmas Day, there's a big air battle over Puget Sound and our navy knocks out a dozen Zero planes and saves the fleet." And everyone gets a medal in a special White House ceremony, I added to myself.

"Okay," he said. "Not boring."

"You bet." For a minute we didn't talk. Then, "I've been thinking maybe we could do something together. For the war effort."

His face lit up like a Christmas tree. "Oh, Miss Hazel!"

"Just call me Hazel." It was embarrassing, him talking to me like a Japanese houseboy. Even though he was one, sort of.

"Okay. But what can we do?"

"Maybe collect something, if there's anything left to collect. We've pretty much cleaned up all the scrap metal around here. . . . I know! Cooking fat—it's used to make bombs."

His eyes and mouth scrunched up, showing he didn't understand.

"One pound of fat will make two anti-aircraft shells," I explained patiently. "You can use anything—lard, bacon grease. You put it through a strainer and take it to the butcher. My mother must have saved enough to bomb a whole Zero squadron. I'll come over and show you how to do it—would that be all right, you think?"

He nodded again. "Sure! Lula-san likes you. She says you come back anytime."

"Really?" I wasn't sure how much I liked Lula-san, but if I was teaming up with Sogoji, there was probably no avoiding her. "Okay, we'll try it. I'll come over next Saturday afternoon, unless my mother has something for me to do. Is that a deal?"

He nodded happily. "Deal."

12

THE TOWER

When I arrived at the Lanskis', a little before one o'clock next Saturday, the radio was blaring dance music so loud I could hear it through the front door. After knocking hard enough to bruise my knuckles, I turned the knob and eased the door open with a push of my toe. "Hello?" No one answered.

"Hello!" I called again, stepping inside the house. Still no answer. I tiptoed toward the bedroom door, where I got the shock of my life.

Sogoji was beside one of the beds, where Mrs. Lanski lay

facedown. Her dress was unbuttoned, and he was setting fire to her bare back.

"What are you *doing?*" I yelled. He jumped and quickly raked a pile of smoking grass off the lady's back. "Hazel. You're early?"

"Not much. What's going on?"

His hands fluttered like startled sparrows. "When Lula-san has aches and pains, she ask for *yaito*—"

The missus herself slowly turned her head. "Why, Hazel. Sogoji said you might be over today. Good to see you, honey."

Sometimes you feel like the whole world has flipped over without you—or that you've flipped, all by yourself. I couldn't think of a thing to say.

Sogoji pointed to a tin tray lying on a table on the other side of Mount Lula-san. On the tray was a smoking pile of bird's nest—at least, that's what it looked like. "Wormwood moss," he said.

"Huh?"

Mrs. Lanski yawned. "It's a Japanese trick."

"But what's it *for?*"

"A few years back, when I had that meningitis, Sogoji's daddy offered to try it on me. How it works is, he sets these little piles of wormwood moss on the spots where my back aches and lights these little fires just until the moss warms up, and it takes the ache right away. These Japs know a thing or two about doctoring. Ask Sogoji to try it on you sometime."

"I . . . don't have a backache."

"Course not. Enjoy your youth; it'll never come again." Mrs. Lanski yawned again, making her curly locks quiver. "That's good, Sogoji; thanks a bunch. You two run along now." She closed her eyes and nestled into the mattress.

He covered her with a sheet and eased around the bed, holding the smoking tray. I followed him into the kitchen, still speechless. He set the tray on the stove top and picked up an iron skillet. "Fried chicken for dinner! Lotta fat."

"Uh-huh." I took a breath. "Where did your father learn that—what do you call it?"

"*Yaito.* My father learned from his father. It passes down, father to son." The old anxious look crossed his face, as if he were afraid of what I was thinking. "It does good, not harm."

"Lula-san sure seems to think so. It's just . . ." *Strange,* I thought: odd and foreign and totally outside anything I knew. Just when Sogoji was starting to feel more comfortable, he had to go and do something like this. In the bedroom, the dance music ended. The announcer's voice crackled, "That was Artie Shaw's band, with 'Moonlight and Shadows.' Now we go to NBC news. The Pacific fleet—" A loud click shut him off.

"Look!" Sogoji scooped an egg out of the sink. At least, that's what it appeared to be, a little flattened on top.

"What is it?"

"It's . . . an anti-aircraft *shell.*" His eyebrows jumped up almost to his bangs.

What now? I thought, stepping closer. The top of the shell had been carefully cut off and filled to the brim with creamy lard, just beginning to set. "Say again?"

"An anti-aircraft—"

"SHELL! I get it! I mean—it's a joke, right?" He nodded, then laughed. It was the oddest laugh I'd ever heard, a dry crickety "chk-chk-chk." It was funnier than the joke, so I joined in.

Feeling close to normal again, I helped him clean up the kitchen and cook down some pork scraps he'd saved. We ended up with two pounds of fat, strained into empty tin cans. Then we sat at the table and he showed me how to make birds from folded paper—another Japanese trick.

"Good day's work?" he said. I think he meant it as a statement, but it sounded like a question.

"Uh-huh. I was hoping for more than two pounds of fat, though."

"We take too much, Lula-san might notice."

I ran my thumbnail along a fold to make a sharp crease. "It wouldn't hurt her to give a little more to the war effort."

"Besides Jed, you mean?"

My thumbnail stopped in its track. Maybe Mrs. Lanski couldn't admit there was a war on because she had so much to lose in it. More than my mother, even. "Well . . . she didn't want him to go."

"No. Very, very unhappy. Dark days around here. For me, too."

"Did Jed ever take you fishing or anything like that?"

"No, can't take me anyplace. Too careful I'd be seen. But he teached me how to be useful 'round here—work wood, make repairs."

"Uh-huh." I was remembering how much Jed had wanted to join the marines—how every time a military plane flew overhead, he would stop what he was doing and stare at it until it was out of sight. Had he wanted to go so much that he'd trained Sogoji to take his place? I rubbed my hand on the outside of my pocket where the silver dollar was—a habit now, whenever I thought of Jed. "Listen," I said, "we've got to do everything we can to help the war effort so he can come home safe."

"Right." He nodded so hard his hair bounced.

"Did you say Jed taught you carpentry?"

"Right. We build a new chicken coop last winter."

"Swell." I dug the stub of a pencil from my bib pocket, unfolded my paper bird, and started drawing. "A couple of years ago, Frank and I started to build an observation tower on top of the hill. But he's not much of a carpenter." Not much of a finisher, either, I could have added. "We wanted it to look like this." I pushed my sketch to his side of the table. "What do you think?"

Sogoji turned his head to study it from different angles, working his lips in and out and drumming his fingers on the table. "Well?" I asked finally.

"How tall?"

"Fifteen feet? Or maybe twelve."

More drumming, then he said, "It'll take much lumber."

"Yeah, that's the problem. We left some wood up there, and I could probably scrounge a little more, but I thought maybe you—" I stopped, because a peculiar look had come over his face. It reminded me of the Buddha—kind of secretive and sly at the same time.

"Maybe me, yes. Let me show you."

I put my jacket on while he looked in on the lady of the house, still snoozing away. When we were outside, he started down an overgrown path to a place I'd been before: his little shack in the woods. When we arrived, I oohed and aahed like I'd never seen it and wondered if he'd show me the inside.

But without even looking at the house, he trotted on around to the back, explaining, "Before war, Father laid in some wood to build a kitchen shed. But . . ." He didn't finish the sentence.

There was a lean-to behind the house: a mossy, unshingled roof built out from the wall. Underneath it were some rusty wire cages and iron fittings and—I couldn't believe my eyes—a stack of uncut two-by-twos and two-by-fours, set on log struts to keep them off the wet ground.

"Behold!" he said, and behold I did. My tower dream had come true.

*　*　*

It was almost dark that evening when Estelle danced in from an afternoon at the Red Cross. "We're taking back the Philippines!"

"I heard it on the radio." Mom pulled a blouse from the stack of laundry she was ironing and smoothed it across the board. "Just because we beat them on the water doesn't mean they'll give up on land."

"Oh, Mom." Estelle pulled a red rose from her hair and twirled it around her head. "The Yanks are coming! It won't be long now."

I looked up from the *Boy's Backyard Building Book* that I'd dug out from under Frank's bed. To tell the truth, I wasn't sure I was ready for the war to be over yet. I had a tower to build, so I could spot an enemy plane and get a medal pinned on me by President Roosevelt.

"Where did the rose come from?" Mom asked.

"From Peyton's Floral, naturally. It's a victory rose."

Mom set the iron on its stand, turned the blouse, and damped it down with the sprinkler bottle. "Hmm. I guess the war can't last long now that Lula Lanski has pitched in. She gave Hazel two pounds of fat from her kitchen today."

"No kidding? You deserve a medal, sis."

"You'll have to be sure and tell Jed about it in your next letter." Mom snapped a sleeve flat on the board, not looking up.

"Will do."

"Preferably tonight. He may wonder why you're not writing so often."

"At ease, Mother—"

"You know I'm not wild about your . . . understanding with him, but while he's doing his part, you should do yours."

"Message received." Estelle swept on to the bathroom, crying out, "I shall return!"

Mom looked toward the bathroom with a frown but didn't volunteer what the frown was about.

Since Uncle Chet didn't need me so much now, I could spend every spare hour on our new project. I found the plan that Frank had wanted to use: a "Cascade Fire Tower" in three tiers with a ranger's hut on top. We could do without the hut. After some survey work, we decided that if we built just west of the spruce trees, the tower could be twelve feet tall without anyone noticing from the Lanski house.

Getting that wood all the way to Hawk's Nest was the hardest part, but Sogoji found Jed's old toy wagon, knocked off both ends, and oiled the wheels so we could use it for transport. I pulled and he pushed, and unlike my brother, he didn't give up easy.

We made some progress every day that week. Sogoji worked fast to get his housework done in the morning, and once Lula-san was bedded down, he headed for the hill. If I couldn't come, he brought a saw and cut wood to fit our blueprint. On Saturday we carried up our last load of lumber and had an official groundbreaking. After setting four posts in the holes he dug and securing the two-by-two stringers along the top with rusty nails, I poured a little root beer at each corner. Then we split the rest between two jelly glasses. A chilly November breeze burrowed through my jacket, but getting so much done in such a short time gave me a glowy feeling inside. "To the Columbia watchtower!" I said, raising my glass.

"To victory!" he replied.

I turned south. "To Mount Hood!"

"To Fuji-san!" He waved west.

"Fuji-san? You mean Mount Fuji?"

He nodded. "In pictures I see, he looks like Hood."

"I guess so. Why do you call it Fuji-san, like it's a person?"

"My mother and father say Fujiyama is more than a mountain—he's the spirit of Japan."

"Oh." My idea of the spirit of Japan was sneak attacks, not snowy peaks. "Hey! Is that the mountain on the card that's in your—"

I broke off, realizing I'd just admitted to trespassing in his house. Now you've done it, stupid! I waited for him to be hurt, or mad, or sorry he had ever made friends with me. Then he would gather up his tools and haul them down the hill and never come up here again.

But Sogoji just stared off in the direction of Mount Hood, his face smooth and polite. I was wondering if he'd even heard me, but then he said, "The wedding card? In Father's house?"

"Uh-huh." I took a deep breath, feeling miserable. "See ... I thought you might be a spy. So when Mr. Lanski said you had a house by the creek, I thought I'd better go have a look in case you had a radio or something, and of course you don't, but I had to look and I saw the pictures. . . ."

It all sounded pretty dumb to me now, and I waited for him to say so. But he just sat down on the apple crate we were using for a sawhorse, with an expression more sad than mad. "A spy?"

"Yeah, it was silly." I plopped down beside him. "I'm really sorry for trespassing. It's just that—well, you look so Japanese. Not that you can help it—"

"I am Japanese," he said simply. "Like mother and father. But American, too."

"I know, Sogoji. . . . But there's a war on and we can't be too careful." After a pause, I said, "I thought your mother looked nice."

His face brightened. "Yes. That's her bride photo."

"You mean a wedding picture? Where's the groom?"

"No, I mean she was a picture bride. When Japanese men come here, there was no woman to marry. So a man wrote to his hometown and sent picture of himself, asking if any young girls want to marry such a handsome, well-to-do fellow. Girls who want to come to America, they send pictures in return for the man to choose the one he likes."

"So your father was already working here . . . and your mother was in Japan, and they decided to marry each other just from looking at each other's picture?" He nodded. "What if a girl came over and decided she didn't like the man?"

"It's a very bad shame to go back. The girl's family would have trouble getting rid of her after. Most men would think, too bouncy." He waved his hand like a ball flipping back and forth.

"Well, at least your mother stayed, or you wouldn't be here. Was she happy?"

He looked down, and his glance slewed to one side. By now I knew what that meant—we'd stumbled over a subject he would like to change. After an awkward pause, I changed it. "Well, back to work, huh? You think we can get this thing finished in another week?"

13

TENGU-KAKUSHI

Progress at school wasn't as good as on the hill, but by the second week in November the playwriting committee had finished a script. Except the ending. We were split down the middle over whether the soldier in the family ought to show up at the end of the play. Sherman and I said no, Gladys and Ivy said yes yes *please yes.* Margie, the committee chairman, couldn't make up her mind. On the one hand (as she pointed out almost every day), everybody liked a happy ending. But on the other hand, having the soldier waltz onstage at that particular moment, just in time for Christmas, wasn't very realistic. And the community had seen four boys go off to war who would never come back—the blue stars on their banners had been replaced by gold. Would those gold star mothers feel their loss was being taken lightly?

"Still," Ivy said on Monday, "the play ought to have the soldier *in* it. Maybe he could just stand offstage like he's on shipboard and sing, 'I'll Be Home for Christmas.'"

"That's dumb," Sherman said.

"Oh, *you*. No matter what I said, you'd call it dumb. What do you think, Hazel? Hazel?"

I was only listening with half a mind. The other half was on Jed's unnamed Pacific island, where I'd made a great discovery: a Japanese who was raised by American missionaries and turned out to be on our side! We made a great team, because once I had located the enemy hideout, my Faithful Japanese Companion (or FJC for short) translated their overheard plans. We had started building an outpost in the jungle for sending radio signals.

Ivy's question pulled me away just as the FJC and I were figuring out how to fix the antenna on our tower: "Hazel! What about having the soldier stand off to one side and sing?"

I blinked. "No boy in this school can carry a tune."

"We could play a record. He could be wounded, with his arm in a sling. Or he could lean on a crutch and look sad."

Sherman rolled his eyes, but Margie sat up straight and grabbed the sides of her desk. "I know!"

"Calm down, for crying out loud." Sherman's eyes darted to the front of the room, where Mr. Mayhew sat with his feet on the desk, reading a *National Geographic* he had borrowed from the Hedgecocks. While the committee was at work, he could assign compositions to the rest of the class and take the afternoon easy.

Margie leaned forward and lowered her voice. "Here's my idea. At the end of the play, the door opens and the soldier walks in, but he's got a bad limp and he's favoring his right leg. His *right leg*—get it? That's where he took the shrapnel when he was on Guadalcanal."

Sherman snorted. "I hope they can get him to talk about it, unlike some people. My brother's a reporter for the newspaper—"

"Not like you don't tell us every other day," Ivy muttered.

"—and he's been trying to get an interview with Mr. Mayhew for a month. But the guy's as tight-lipped as—"

"But don't you see?" Margie demanded. "The soldier in our play *is* Mr. Mayhew. We can't call him Arthur, but everybody will figure out it's him, and his mother in the play can say how proud she is, and the neighbors can come over and tell him they appreciate his sacrifice and wah-la!" Margie spread her hands. "He gets a tribute before he even knows what hit him!"

Ivy and Gladys squealed with excitement, and even Sherman grinned. I had to admit it was pretty smart. "If we do that," I said, "maybe I won't have to give a speech." My mother's original quiet-little-plaque idea had grown to a formal presentation with a statement that Mom decided should be given by me. I was dreading it already.

"Of course you'll have to give a speech." Margie was scribbling notes on her memo pad. "The school board can't just *throw* that plaque at him. There has to be a presentation. But our surprise ending will set everybody up for it—that is, if we're all agreed."

We all agreed, and the next order of business was to make sure the audience got the point. Suggestions came thick and fast, with everybody whispering so the teacher wouldn't hear: "Marvin could play him—he's almost as tall, and he's got the same color hair." "Maybe we could sneak his uniform! Mrs. Hedgecock could swipe it for us and say she sent it to the cleaners. . . ." "Whoever plays him has to practice how he walks. . . ." "We could show him thumbing a ride to Hood River."

When Ivy mentioned this, the other girls broke out in giggles. "Do you know what I'm talking about?" Ivy asked me with a smug look.

"No . . . Should I?"

"Uhhhh-huh. Mr. Mayhew's been hitchhiking to Hood River at least twice a week."

"So?"

"*So?* He's going to see your sister. He's been spotted sweet-talking her at the bank."

A snaky feeling suddenly coiled up in my stomach. "So?" I said again, but my voice sounded limp as a string.

"We don't mean there's anything bad going on," Margie put in. "I think it's nice he's coming out of his shell. But people *are* starting to talk, since she seemed to be pretty serious about Jed Lanski." Margie stopped shuffling papers and looked at me, as though I could give her the lowdown. But I couldn't manage anything more than a shrug. Was this the reason Estelle had slacked off on letter writing?

"Of course, nobody would blame her if she broke up with Jed," Ivy said, sounding like her mom. "He's nice, but his mother and dad—"

"Could we finish this darn play?" Sherman pleaded. "You can gossip on your own time."

So what if people were talking? I thought. People talked all the time, and half of what they said, in my opinion, didn't amount to much. If a fellow wanted to take Estelle out for a Coke now and then, it wasn't anybody's business, especially if the fellow was a veteran wounded in the service of his country. Being nice to him was the least Estelle could do . . . wasn't it?

Was that what she was doing when she came in late two nights that week? The first time she blamed it on missing her ride, and the second time was because she'd decided to do some last-minute shopping. Both might be true, but only halfway. What if Estelle missed her ride because she was out dancing with Mr. Mayhew? Or the shopping was for jewelry, like an engagement ring? She did write to Jed one night, but the letter was only one page.

I didn't know what to think. Of course I wanted them to break up, but was this a good time? As plain as a "Terry and the Pirates" comic strip, I saw Jed on his Pacific island receiving a cruel, one-page letter from Estelle:

JED (*reading, with dismayed look*): "Dear Jed, I am sorry to tell you that . . ."

COMPANY SERGEANT: Heads up, men! We're moving out!

JED (*thinking*): No! It can't be. . . .

MARINE BUDDY: Say, Jed, what's eating you?

JED: It's a letter . . . from my girl. . . . She says . . .

MARINE BUDDY (*clapping him on shoulder*): Found somebody else, eh? Tough luck, pal! But there's more than one fish in the sea!

JED (*thinking*): No! There's no other girl for me—

SERGEANT: Japs over the next hill! They're firing on our planes! Let's go get 'em!

JED (*thinking, as sweat breaks out on forehead*): Got to pull myself together . . . But life doesn't seem worth living anymore. . . .

No! I felt like busting out of jungle concealment and throwing my arms around him. Just wait a few years and you can get secretly engaged to me!

*   *   *

A few days later, we pounded some two-by-fours across the first tier of our observation tower to make a platform, then started on the second level. I was handing some boards up to Sogoji when one of them slipped and hit me on the foot. After I'd finished yelling and hopping around on the other foot, Sogoji asked, "Does something worry you?"

"Why do you say that?" I gasped.

He smiled, and hooked his hammer claw over a crossbeam. "You act like *tengu-kakushi.*"

"Tangoo who?"

"Not who, what." He squatted on the platform. "The *tengu* are like—how would you say—fairies? Heavenly dog, the Japanese say."

"Heavenly dogs?" I climbed up beside him. "You mean, spirits?"

"*Hai!* I mean, yeah, like spirits. You find them in hills and forests. They look a little like bird, a little like human."

"So you call them heavenly *dogs*? That makes a lot of sense."

"They enjoy tricks on humans. Sometime the *tengu* steal away a man or woman and hide them awhile. Once they carried off Kintaro's mother. He searched fifty days and nights, through fogs and over mountaintops, riding the back of a mountain lion. Finally he found the *tengu* hiding place and fought their king to win his mother back. A good thing, because if he don't rescue her, she'd come back on her own, only—" Sogoji made his head wobble and his eyes roll back.

"She'd be crazy?" He nodded. "I'm not *that* far gone."

"No, no, you're just gone. *Tengu-kakushi* means 'hidden by the *tengu*.' I go to rescue you, see?" He grinned.

"Thanks. Now maybe you should go after my sister." Next minute, I was pouring out the whole problem of Estelle and Mr. Mayhew and people talking. I even mentioned the engagement to Jed, which of course I wasn't supposed to. It felt a little funny, sharing family secrets with him, but after it was out, I felt like I had just let go of a load of bricks.

Sogoji listened thoughtfully, his lips tucked in and his eyes closed almost to slits. For a few minutes we just sat, swinging our legs and watching the sun slip another notch toward the horizon. "Estelle is a nice girl," he said then. "I like her."

"But you've never met her."

"I saw. Heard her talk. Through the kitchen door."

"That's not enough to get to know somebody. I'll admit she's nice, but she's kind of flighty, too."

"Flighty?" He made the word sound a little like *frighty*.

"You know. In the head. She might be thinking she doesn't want to be engaged after all, or at least not to somebody so far away. It would help if Jed wrote more often, but I guess he can't. So if the *tengu*s have kidnapped her, there's nobody to— Hey, wait a minute! You said Kintaro went to save his mother, but I thought his mother died when he was born. Isn't that the way you told the story first?"

He looked both startled and confused. "No! I mean, lots of

Kintaro stories. Some say this, some say that." He sprang up like a grasshopper. "Come on—we'll get these boards nailed by sunset, yes?"

I found myself watching Estelle closely for the next few days, as though looking for signs of *tengu-kakushi*. But she was late only on Friday afternoon and had a forthright explanation when Mom asked why: "To tell you the truth, Hazel's teacher showed up at closing time and offered to buy me a cup of coffee and a slice of coconut pie."

"Is that all it was?"

"Mother. You're the one who said he should get out more. We sat right by the front window of Pop's Coffee Shop, in plain view of the whole town, and nobody saw anything worth talking about. I was just being neighborly—besides, I picked up the check."

So that was all right. I erased the "Dear John" episode of Jed's story and substituted another where Jed received a perfumy note filled with I-love-yous and XXXXXs—after which he charged a Jap machine-gun nest and took it out single-handed. When he received his Medal of Honor, I wasn't sure whether it was Estelle or me standing beside him, but for now that didn't matter.

14

THE HONOR OF THE EMPEROR

Estelle and I spent all of Saturday morning taking out props from under the apple trees and storing them away in the tractor shed. When we got home, there was a pot of soup on the stove and a letter from Jed propped against the lamp on the end table, like a king on a throne. Mom left it there before dashing off to hand out ration coupons at the community hall.

Estelle swooped down on the envelope and ripped it open. Whatever was in it didn't cause her to jump up and down like the first one did. She read it at least twice, then sighed and glanced at me. "I guess you want to know what it says."

"Well, do *tell.*"

"Okay: 'Hi, babe, these last two weeks I've been on the water headed for—' That part's blocked out, of course. 'I thought I signed up for the marines, not the navy. Sea life is a great way to make friends. Nothing like hurling your cookies during a storm with eight hundred of your bosom buddies, ha ha. The food leaves a lot to be desired. I'd give anything to sit down to a meal of your mom's meat loaf—or even *my* mom's meat loaf. Seriously, we've seen some action. Last Thursday the Japs attacked our convoy near an island I can't name—'"

Estelle paused. "That part's blocked out for a few lines." She cleared her throat. "'Anyway,' he says, 'this will be short and sweet because I've been called for cleanup detail. That's me— ever ready to defend my country with a mop and a bucket, ha ha. Keep your chin up, kid. And keep writing. Nothing brightens my day like a letter from you.'

"'My best wishes to Hazel and your mom.'"

I sat there for a while, then asked, "I guess he didn't stick a note in for me this time?"

She checked the envelope again. "Nope." After a pause, she added, "I think I'll write him before lunch. Do you want to?"

I nodded, even though he hadn't mentioned that a letter from *me* would brighten his day. Of course he was busy and distracted, defending his country and all. So I could forgive him. But I still wished he could have spared a word for me instead of lumping me and Mom together in his "best wishes."

While Estelle curled up on the sofa with her stationery box, I went to my room and tore a page out of my logbook—which I hadn't used much since we got so busy on the tower. *Dear Jed, I've been getting to know Charlie. We're doing something for the war effort—wait till you see it. At school we're putting on a play about a soldier who gets to come home for Christmas. It's mostly dumb—the play is, I mean. But I wish the soldier was you. I know you want to stay until you finish the job, so* . . .

What to say next? I kept seeing him on the deck of a battleship, blazing away with an anti-aircraft gun at Zero planes. . . . *so finish the job soon and come home,* I wrote finally. *Your friend, Hazel.*

All of a sudden I was really, truly ready for the war to be over, whether I got a medal out of it or not.

After a quiet lunch with Estelle, I pulled my jacket on again and headed for Hawk's Nest. On the way I tried to imagine what I could do for Jed on a battleship. There wasn't much. On land I could at least scout for him—even now, climbing the hill, I skirted from bush to bush so I could sneak up to our hidden tower and scout for Japanese planes or spies. "If there's a Jap within fifty miles," the marines liked to say, "Hazel can find him." Nearing the top, I slowed down to listen. Sure enough, my ears picked up the sound of a hammer. Under cover of the noise I crept closer and soon had the FJC in view before he suspected my presence.

Then I shouted in surprise: "Hey!" Sogoji had almost finished the second tier—the framework was all in place and he was pounding a two-by-four across the top stringers. "How long have you been here?"

He looked up. "Couple hours. See how much I did."

"Didn't you have to cook dinner or get Lula-san settled for a nap or anything?"

"No. Not today." He was concentrating real hard on getting one end of the board at just the right angle. "She's not feeling good."

"How come? Did she catch a cold, or—"

"Letter came. From Jed." Bang! Bang! Bang! One long nail sank into the wood.

"Yeah, we got one, too. What did he say? How did he sound?"

"I dunno. I don't get to read." He set the other nail and started pounding.

"Sogoji, put that hammer down for a minute, wouldja?" He paused for a second, then squatted on the first-tier platform like a monkey. "What's up with Lula-san?"

He couldn't quite look at me. His glance darted here and there as though searching out a place to hide. "Letters from Jed make her all upset. She forgets herself, throws things sometimes. Lanski-san says it's better if I make myself scarce awhile."

"Oh." I couldn't think of anything else to say.

"Tomorrow—tonight, even, she'll remember her shoulder hurts or she'd like some chicken potpie. Then it's okay again."

"I see."

After a minute he said, "We make good progress here. Let's keep going, okay?"

We got to work, and since all I had to do was hammer down the boards he cut, my mind was free to consider Mrs. Lanski. Maybe it just got too hard to pretend that Jed was away on a South Sea cruise. Maybe sometimes the truth crashed through that door she was trying to hold shut and reminded her that Jed was in a place where he could get killed. By a Jap. And then she'd look at Sogoji and see . . . a Jap.

Suddenly I turned on the board I'd just nailed down and saw . . . Sogoji. Just himself, not a grinning fiend in a cartoon with buckteeth and glasses. I didn't realize I was holding my breath until it rushed out in a sigh of relief.

He glanced up from his sawing. "What is it?"

"Aren't you tired? You've been working three hours straight. Let's take a break."

He finished cutting the board and climbed up to the two-by-four I was sitting on. The second tier was done, except for the platform, and we were perched almost eight feet above the ground. I was amazed at what even that much elevation could do. "I'll bet when we get the top finished, we can see all the way to Portland."

"May not be able to finish," he said. "Running out of wood."

"What?" I gasped. "But we've got to!"

He pointed down at our wood supply, which had gotten

awfully small without me noticing. "Only one more two-by-four. The rest, it may be enough to finish framework, maybe not. And we still need a ladder to climb up and boards across top to stand on."

"Then we'll scrounge if we have to. We can find enough scrap wood, I know we can."

"Why, Hazel? We've got a good tower already."

"Not good enough. We planned it to be *twelve feet*—I mean—" I was close to tears all of a sudden.

"Hazel-san?" His voice was soft. His hand hovered over my arm but never fell. "What's wrong?"

I brushed a sleeve across my nose. "It's just that . . . I made a promise to Jed. He asked me to watch out for things around here. Look—" I pulled the silver dollar out of my pocket. "He gave me this, to remind me."

Sogoji stared at the coin, as though it were a sacred relic. "Did he say what you watch for?"

"To look after his mom and dad—but you, too. I think he was hoping we'd meet. Anyway, he asked, and I promised, and it's like if I do my part, he'll be safe. And finishing the tower—I don't know, it's like . . . if we don't, maybe he won't be safe. That's silly, right?"

His hands were restlessly squeezing his knee and scratching his ear and propping him up while he shifted on the narrow board. Now one finger came down on the silver dollar for a second. "We'll finish. One way or 'nother."

Scrounging wasn't easy, though. I spent the next few days poking around the orchard sheds until Uncle Chet asked me what was up. When I told him what I was looking for, he just said, "Tough luck. I've got to replace some wood in the barn this winter and don't know where it's coming from. Lumber's as scarce as everything else."

Finally I pried some of the shelving out of the garage, hoping nobody would miss it since we didn't go in there much. With that and a few pieces Sogoji found, we could finish the sides of the third tier. Late on Tuesday afternoon, I hauled my contribution up the hill, hoping for an early dismissal on Wednesday so we'd have time to use it.

Mr. Mayhew didn't let me down. The next day he dismissed us at two, early enough to squeeze an hour and a half of daylight if I hurried. Mom was still at Citizens' League when I got home, so I dashed to the bedroom to change clothes and be out of the house before she returned. While pulling up my overall straps, I happened to notice that Jed's last letter was open on Estelle's dressing table, weighted with a perfume bottle. Something struck me about it: it seemed longer than what I remembered Estelle reading.

Slowly I moved the bottle aside. Without touching the letter—it seemed less sneaky that way—I found the place where he'd written *an island I can't name.* Estelle had said that the next part was blocked out, but before that he'd written, *That was my first experience with the kamikaze pilots. You may have read about them— it's a new tactic. They take some kind of vow to the emperor to cripple our ships by crashing planes into them. It's kind of hard on the nerves, knowing they won't stop. One guy I saw—*

Heavy black bars covered the next three lines. I tried to guess what happened to the guy he saw: took a direct hit that blew him to pieces? Went batty and jumped overboard? Jed survived, or he wouldn't be writing the letter, but he seemed pretty shook up: *To tell you the truth, I never was very chatty with the Man Upstairs, but please put in a good word for me. We've never fought a tougher enemy. Keep that to yourself, though—no point in undermining morale.*

I fought down the lump in my throat. It hurt a little that he'd share his fears with Estelle and not with me—didn't think I was tough enough to take it, probably. To him I was just a kid. Well, never mind—I'd show him.

Sogoji was already at Hawk's Nest when I got there. Without saying much, we nailed the top stringers in place and laid our last two-by-four across to hold them together. "What now?" I asked.

He hopped up to perch on the board, swinging his legs. The heavy clouds had started to leak a cold drizzle. "Some view up here."

"But it's not doing us much good if we don't have a platform to stand on," I snapped. Without that, the tower looked pointless, like a pump without a handle or a bird without a wing. Just looking at it made me mad—so close to the end, and we still couldn't finish.

"We'll think some more, find solution." He went on swinging his legs, looking around like a sightseer passing the time—or like he didn't care if we finished the project or not. "Kintaro built a tower one time."

That's all I need now, I thought: a fairy tale.

"One time the emperor's beautiful wife turned very sick, almost to die. The doctors say she will die if she don't get a dose of moonbeams to lift her spirit. She is a great-great-great-great-grandchild of the sun, just like the emperor, so her best medicine comes from the sky. Please, Kintaro, the emperor says, can anything be done to help my beloved empress? Kintaro puzzles and puzzles over problem, finally hits upon a plan. He asks his friends to help—cheetah, monkey, ape, eagle. Together they cut down tall pines and haul logs to Fuji-san's peak and build the tallest tower in the world. On the night of the first full moon, Kintaro climbs the tower with a golden jar and traps moonbeams to take back to court. And there the beautiful empress, daughter of the sun, pulls the cork of the golden jar and the air is full of moonbeams that make her well."

"So all we need are some animals to help us cut down trees," I grumbled. Japanese stories were a little too neat and pretty, even though the Japs themselves weren't. Judging by Jed's letter, a lot of them were maniacs.

"If I was like Kintaro," he said, "the animals would do it."

"What happened to him in the end?"

"In the end of what, Hazel?"

"The end of the stories. How did he die?"

"Kintaro never died! He became one of the immortals!"

"Oh, I'll bet. He probably killed himself."

Sogoji jumped down beside me. His face turned a little ashy, as though he'd just heard terrible news. "Why you say that?"

"Because that's what the great Japanese warriors do, isn't it? Like Kintaro's father, killing himself for shame? Like the kamikazes, killing themselves for the emperor?"

"No! Only when there's some good reason. When duty demands—"

"Duty, my foot!" My anger surprised even me. "It's nobody's duty to commit suicide. What good are you when you're dead?"

The color was coming back to his face but draining from his voice. "Sometime it's the way of honor. The only way."

"Well, I think it's nuts." I squirmed out between the trussed boards and dropped to the ground. "Absolutely *nuts*!"

Sogoji looked down at me, biting his lip and clenching his hands on the stringer boards. "The kamikaze—they're like samurai. They will sacrifice everything for honor, for emperor—"

"Americans will sacrifice for America, too, but our motto is 'Live to fight another day.' Suicide pilots are nuts. They're just— I know, maybe they're *tengu*-whatever. Captured by the *tengu* and their brains are scrambled." I staggered around like I was drunk. "Hey, men, I've got a great idea. Let's go crash a few dozen perfectly good Zero planes into an American aircraft carrier!"

When I'd turned a full circle, he was on the ground, gathering up tools and stuffing them in a potato sack. The look on his face sobered me up fast. "So," I asked, "what should we do now?"

"I am done." He swung the bag over his shoulder and started for the rim of the hill, and it occurred to me I'd gone too far.

"How are we going to finish this tower?" I called after him.

His shoulders went up and down, but he didn't stop.

"C'mon, Sogoji! I didn't mean to hurt your feelings."

At the edge of the clearing he turned around, his face perfectly still. He put both hands together and bowed—very formal, very Japanese. Then he adjusted the bag of tools on his shoulder and plunged into the rhododendron thicket.

As his head and shoulders disappeared from view, I shouted, "You shouldn't be so thin-skinned when there's a war on!"

15

A White Dove

I thought he'd get over it. Soon enough he'd forget the argument and one of us would figure out how to make an observation platform, and we'd finish the tower and start some serious air-patrol work. The following Saturday, I ran up to Hawk's Nest with the field glasses, in spite of a steady rain, and stayed long enough that he must have seen me if he was watching. But he never came, and the tower looked so sad and abandoned I didn't even want to climb it.

On Monday after school I went up again, but my area surveillance felt gloomy and pointless. When I got back home,

Mom was sitting in the swivel chair at her desk, talking on the phone. "What do you mean? They won't let you off for *Thanksgiving?* Not even for *one day?* . . . I know about the production quota, but if they can't do without one machinist for one day, we're in a sorry state. . . . I'm *trying* to, Howard, but this is ridiculous. When Frank called Saturday, he said he probably wouldn't even be home for Christmas, just New Year's. . . . Yes, they want to finish that armory project in Gresham. . . ."

I hurried to get my rain boots off, but next minute she said, "All right. I'll tell your mother. Yes, of course you can call on Thursday. Goodbye." She hung up and put her head in her hands.

"I wanted to talk to Daddy!" I yelled from the kitchen.

Mom quickly straightened up, then swiveled around to face me. "Well, I'm sorry. I didn't know you were there. He was just calling to say he can't meet us at Grandma's for Thanksgiving. He'll try to get an extra day at Christmas."

"Huh." I started toward the bedroom, still mad.

"Just a minute, Hazel. I wrote your presentation speech—listen to this." She picked up a stenographer's pad and began to read: "'In this season of peace and goodwill our thoughts turn to those who must think of war. . . .'" The speech went on about sacrifices and hope for the future and wishing to recognize those who valued their country more than life: "'. . . and so we are honored to present you, Corporal Arthur Mayhew, with this small token of our esteem in recognition of your faithful service,' et cetera. What do you think?"

"I think it's just what Mr. Mayhew said he didn't want."

"I know that's what he *said,* but I doubt it's what he really means. What do you think of the speech itself?"

"It's way too long to memorize! Even without the et cetera."

"That will only be a few more words. And it's *not* too long to memorize. When I was your age, I memorized 'Hiawatha,' 'The Concord Hymn,' and 'Paul Revere's Ride' in one semester."

"Well, maybe if you wrote it in rhyme—"

She slapped down the stenographer's pad and took a deep breath. "I'm not arguing with you, Hazel. You will say the speech, and that's that. But—" I could see her doing her part to be more cheerful. "Wait until you see the goods I picked up for your Christmas dress. I think I can make it in time for the program."

She had found a bargain in dark green taffeta with pale wavy highlights woven into it. I fell in love at first sight but didn't love the plans she had for a ruffly white organza pinafore to go over it. "Pinafores are for little girls!"

"No, they aren't. It'll be darling on you." Just like a mother: one minute claiming you were too old to act like a little girl and the next minute wanting to dress you up like one.

We were still arguing when Estelle came home, and since it was her kind of argument, she jumped right in. "I'm with Hazel, Mom. Forget the organza and the ruffles. A nice simple dress with a full skirt and lace collar might even last her through next year."

"Fine. Next year she can just leave off the pinafore."

"She'll be twelve in a couple of weeks, you know. Next stop, thirteen. That's the way it goes."

"But it doesn't have to go so fast!"

Even though they were talking about me like I wasn't there, I was feeling pretty friendly toward Estelle, until she opened her purse. While she was feeling around for a stick of chewing gum, an envelope heaved up from the cluttered depths. There was no address on it, just a name, with some extra words, like *angel.* The handwriting, so neat it could have come out of a copybook, was the same that spelled out *Good work!* on my spelling tests at school.

Estelle caught me looking and snapped the purse shut, her cheeks blooming like a red, red rose. "Anyway, that's my advice. I'll let you wear my gold locket with your new dress, Hazel."

"You mean the one with Jed's picture in it?"

The red shade grew deeper, but Estelle didn't answer.

Sogoji hadn't shown up for a whole week and I thought it was ridiculous to take hurt feelings so far. I'd really done him a favor; with a war on, it wouldn't do to get sentimental about the enemy. Sure, it was tough, to find your country at war with your own people. But the best way to deal with life's hard knocks, as Daddy said, was to develop an alligator's hide over a lamb's heart. My heart felt soft and lambish enough—if Sogoji wanted to be friends again, I'd let bygones be bygones.

That's what I was thinking on my way home from school

that Wednesday. Just before my drive, where the road curves to go up to the Lanskis' house, I met their rusty black pickup coming down. Mr. Lanski raised a hand to me and rolled on by, then stopped. I heard the rev of a motor backing up as he pulled even with me and cranked the window down. "Hey there."

I blinked in surprise. "Hi, Mr. Lanski."

"I'm going down to dig the last potatoes. You want to come?"

He never asked for help from anybody. There could be only one reason: he wanted to talk to me. I said, "Let me change my clothes."

Five minutes later, I was sitting in the front seat as he coasted down the road. He shifted into low gear to bump into his north field, where I used to pick melons with Jed. I helped him unload the wheelbarrow, shovel, and rake from the pickup bed and we toted them over to the potato patch. Taking the shovel, he started digging up hills while I raked the dirt off and tossed potatoes in the wheelbarrow. "So," he said at last, "did you and Sogoji have a fight or what?"

I figured this was coming. "Yes, sir. He's awful touchy."

"What was it about?"

"It was dumb! He's always telling these stories about Kintaro—do you know Kintaro?" Mr. Lanski shook his head. "He's a big strong Japanese hero, like Hercules, I guess. Sogoji's mother used to tell him these stories, and I think he made up some on his own just because he was lonely. Anyway, all I did was ask if Kintaro killed himself."

"Humph," Mr. Lanski said.

"Then we got into a big argument about kamikaze pilots and the honor of the emperor and all that stuff. I told him he ought to start thinking like an American, and he got all snotty and Japanese on me."

"Humph," he said again, only this time one corner of his mouth turned up.

"That's what I mean by touchy. I insulted his hero."

Mr. Lanski nodded but turned over two more potato hills before he said anything. "His mother . . . she might've killed herself."

I sat back on my heels, stunned. "What?"

"The Mitsumis had a little farm, and Mr. Mitsumi expected his missus to work as hard as he did on it. Japanese wives do what their husbands say, and I think she tried. But she wasn't very strong. Lost a couple of babies before they finally had Sogoji, and her health was never good. One winter she was down with a fever, and she got out of bed at night and took a long walk and froze to death. I don't know the whole story—she might have been delirious or some such."

His mouth snapped shut, as if it had let too many words out. My mind took a couple of slow somersaults. "Sogoji—he felt pretty close to her, didn't he?"

"Well. . . . He was only about eight years old when it happened."

Not exactly an answer, but I was still putting pieces together. "Was his father mean to him?"

Mr. Lanski dug for at least a minute in silence. It was hard to keep still and wait, but I did. "Mitsumi was . . . a real disappointed man. Things didn't turn out like he'd hoped. Loses his farm, wife goes around the bend, boy don't seem too smart—"

"He *is* smart! He just needed some time."

"I reckon." Mr. Lanski nodded. "But Mitsumi didn't have much to give. It was kind of a shameful thing, what his wife did. There was talk that she wasn't right in the head." (Aha, I thought: *tengu-kakushi!*) "That's why he took the boy and went away for a while. Started hitting the bottle pretty hard, too."

After working in silence for a minute, he added, "Wrecked his liver with all the drinking, I reckon. He died in our kitchen, on a cot. Had a few last words for the boy, which we didn't hear. May have had to do with holding up the honor of the family, or what was left of it."

"That's why Sogoji has those pictures set up in his house!"

"Yep. I didn't have the heart to tell him not to. Just hope the house is so far back in the woods nobody will ever see it. 'Cept you."

I wondered if he knew about my spying expedition. "I never told anybody."

He just nodded, and for a while we worked on without a word. We were getting ready to haul the loaded wheelbarrow back to the pickup when he said, "Sogoji is sort of in between. He's not American, and he's not Japanese. May need a little help figuring out what he is."

I got the idea. Making up our argument was going to be up to me.

But how? I could march over to the Lanskis' and say, "I found out about your mother and dad and now I understand why you're so touchy about suicides and going nuts and everything." But that probably wasn't the best way to go about it.

Thanksgiving at Grandma's was quiet, since neither Daddy nor Frank could get away from work. They called, but that was a lousy substitute. Mom worked too hard to be cheerful, and Estelle didn't even try. My mind wandered, spending the afternoon on Jed's island stalking the enemy with the FJC, who'd been moody lately.

Play rehearsals started the very next week, scheduled for Monday, Wednesday, and Friday afternoons. Margie's mother had typed up copies of our script, with the surprise ending kept from Mr. Mayhew. Since she was directing the play as well as the choir, he just took more naps in the afternoon—even though he called it "grading papers."

On rehearsal days, Mrs. Holmes arrived at one-thirty. First came choir practice with the whole class. Then she dismissed the decorating committee to make paper chains, while the "principals" (as she called the actors) gathered at the front of the room. Margie was Mother—a widow, since none of the boys were willing to play Father. Sherman was Jimmy, the brother, and Susie was the little sister. Owen played Old Mr. Jones, a crotchety neighbor who said "young feller" a lot, while Ivy was the absent soldier's sweetheart and Gladys was Mrs. Gray, the busybody who had just moved in next door. We had to have a nosy neighbor to ask all the background questions. She reminded me of Annie Billings, who lived down the road from us and eavesdropped on our telephone party line.

Marvin would play Arthur Mayhew, alias "Johnny." He didn't want to—didn't want to be in the play at all or even in school, since he'd just turned fifteen and most of his friends were off with the Young America Corps. He was supposed to appear at the back of the room singing the first line of "Watchman, Tell Us of the Night," which would be answered by Petilia singing the second line. But when she heard Marvin sing, Mrs. Holmes decided that Mr. Lance Edmund, who made up the entire bass section of the Methodist church choir, could handle the vocal part while Marvin just limped bravely forward.

I missed being a "principal" because I had to say that darn speech, but Mrs. Holmes made me the prompter. That meant I had to sit up front for rehearsals and hear Margie's opening line over and over: "Here it is Christmas Eve, and we haven't heard a word from Johnny. . . ." For the first week everybody was allowed to use their scripts as they walked through the play, so I didn't have much to do while Mrs. Holmes yelled at the principals: "Don't move in front of Sherman, Petilia!"

Twelve days had gone by since my fight with Sogoji. I had already written at least five notes that I tore up because they sounded stupid. I thought about using our emergency signal—one ring on the telephone, meaning meet me at Hawk's Nest—but wasn't sure what to say when he got there. If he came at all.

"And for heaven's sake," said Mrs. Holmes, "speak UP!"

The last page of the script only had a few lines at the top. I tore them off, leaving a square of white paper, and tried to remember how to fold a bird the way Sogoji had shown me.

Suddenly Owen spoke up as Old Mr. Jones: "We're proud of you, young feller. Because of you, there's a lot fewer filthy Japs livin' and breathin' on God's green earth—"

My head snapped up. "That's not in the script!"

"It oughta be!" Owen shot back. "This is a pantywaist play—it doesn't say anything about the enemy."

Mrs. Holmes paused from moving children around and pushed her hair back, exasperated. "What's the matter, Hazel?"

"Owen's making up lines."

"Darn right. I'm making them *better*."

"What did he say?" Mrs. Holmes was trying to be patient.

"About how there's fewer Japs—Japanese—there's not so many of them now that Johnny's been at war."

"I don't understand," Mrs. Holmes said. "Aren't our boys *trying* to kill Japanese before they kill us?"

"Yes, ma'am, but it's not like they're filthy or . . . anything like that." Sogoji's fingernails were usually cleaner than mine.

"Of course they're filthy!" Owen exclaimed. "And they're sneaky and mean. Ask my cousin how they treated American prisoners in the Philippines. He survived, but none of his buddies did. What are you, a Jap lover?"

"Owen, that doesn't help—" Mrs. Holmes began.

"What are you making, Hazel?" Susie broke in. She left her place onstage and ran over to me. "A bird?"

Slowly I picked it up and raised the wings. The girls all said, "Ooh," and Susie stretched out her hand. "Can I have it?"

I was thinking that if I cut a fringe on the wings, it would look like feathers. "I'll make you another one."

Mrs. Holmes saw her chance. "That's lovely, Hazel. Like a dove of peace. Why don't you go over and teach the decorating committee how to make them, and we'll hang some on the tree? Owen, you'd better stick to the script as written, dear. Let's try it again—"

My ears were still burning at what Owen said, but the "dove of peace" stuck in my mind. It gave me an idea.

16

WHAT ARE FRIENDS FOR?

After getting home from school, I tied a thread to my paper dove and cut out two paper leaves to paste on its beak. They were supposed to look like an olive branch, except I wasn't sure what olive leaves looked like. Mom would probably know, but she was helping out at the Red Cross emergency blood drive. Anyway, a leaf was a leaf. When the work was done, I stared at it for a while, decided it would do, and put on my coat.

Today's mission was so secret and perilous I couldn't take anything that would weigh me down—no knapsack, just the field glasses. Swift and silent, I cut through the woods and climbed the hill, wanting to shush even the twigs that cracked under my feet. On Hawk's Nest, I paused only a moment, not for a general survey but a particular one: to check for any activity around the Lanski house. The yard was empty and the window curtains drawn. The coast was clear. Now for the hard part: rescuing the FJC from enemy hands.

I worked my way down the hill and into the woods, through the tangly jungle where we'd first met and across the path that led to his secret hideout. On the edge of the yard I paused, watching the windows for any twitch of curtains. I was watching so hard I could almost see a Jap sentry patrolling the yard with a rifle on his shoulder.

I waited for him to turn his back—NOW!

Dashing across the yard with the bird in hand, I crouched low and scurried up the porch steps. There was a stretch of telephone line that sagged under the eaves—I could tie the bird to it. It would be a signal for Jed's platoon so they would know where their secret ally was being held. They were scouring the jungle right now; at any minute they could break out with guns blazing. Hurry!

I jumped, trying to fling the thread over the wire, but it wasn't heavy enough to fling. After two more tries I gave up and started wrapping the thread around the support post, heart pounding. The sentry could turn around any minute. Hurry, before—

The back door opened, and Sogoji stood there with a bucket of potato peelings in one hand. We both froze.

The sentry, the platoon, and the blazing guns melted away, leaving just me and Sogoji on the porch. I should have practiced what to say in case this happened—my words fled in panic. I tore the bird away from the post and thrust it at him. "Here! I made it for you, the way you showed me. I'm sorry—and I hope we can be friends again—"

He opened his mouth, but nothing came out. I decided I couldn't wait, but turned and streaked across the yard, melting into the jungle to be well out of range before the marines arrived.

The following Thursday, December 7, I turned twelve without too many people noticing. Mom would bake a cake and Estelle had already bought a present, Daddy would call in the evening and my grandma would send a card. Frank, too, if he remembered. But it would be a miracle if anyone else remembered, what with the black banner on the front page of the newspaper, and speeches broadcast over the radio, and a Pearl Harbor memorial at school, where the boys sang, "You're a Sap, Mr. Jap." Only when I was going out the door that afternoon did Mr. Mayhew say, "Oh, I almost forgot—happy birthday, Hazel."

In the school yard Margie said, "He didn't remember *my* birthday."

"Does that mean you're getting a brother-in-law, Hazel?" Ivy asked, so sweet I could have gagged.

Watching Sherman the German respond to teasing had taught me to keep my mouth shut—not that there was anything to say. Just because Mr. Mayhew was writing notes didn't mean Estelle was encouraging him, but the whole situation felt prickly.

Worse than that, though: three days had passed since my mission, and I hadn't heard a thing from Sogoji. Was he still mad?

When I got home, Mom was frosting a tiny cake in cheerful yellow while a funeral march played over the radio. "Sorry it's so small, but I'm saving sugar for Christmas. How was your day? Did anybody wish you many happy returns?"

"Mr. Mayhew did."

"He did?" Mom's head jerked up. "And how did he know?"

I shrugged, but we both guessed. All she said was, "I washed the beaters already, but do you want to lick the frosting bowl?" I took a seat at the table while she bustled around putting dishes in the sink. Since it was my birthday, I didn't have to do anything, not even answer the phone. Still, when the short *brrring-brrring!* sounded, I jumped for it. Daddy might be calling early. But Mom was on her way out of the kitchen, so she picked it up first. "Hello?"

Then she held the receiver away from her ear, frowning at it. "That's funny. Nobody there. I'm going out to get the clothes off the line. If your father calls, be sure to let me know."

I just nodded, scraping my finger around the bowl. Since

sugar rationing started, Mom never left much, so it took some concentration. The bowl was almost clean enough to see my face in it before I thought about the phone call. Nobody there?

Then it hit me: a signal!

The bowl clattered in the dishpan and I raced to the bedroom to get my overalls on. A few minutes later I tore across the yard, pausing just long enough to yell that I'd be right back. Mom's voice echoed behind me: "Hazel! What in the world—?"

She might have thought there was a whole squad of Jap raiders after me, fast as I was running. The hill slowed me down, but I kept a steady pace, so that when I neared the top, the sight on Hawk's Nest rose before me like a sunrise.

Sogoji had been watching for me. When I appeared, he waved from the top of the tower. The *top* of the tower! All twelve feet of it, where he stood on a firm, steady platform. While I tried to take this in, speechless, he unrolled a flag. It was our old Pearl Harbor flag, tacked on a new pole. He set the pole in the open end of a pipe that ran up from the ground, and the sun-bleached stars and stripes lifted in the evening breeze. "Happy birthday, Hazel!"

My eyes got all misty and my throat closed up. "What—how—"

"Come—let me show you."

I climbed up the ladder of two-by-twos and he gave me a hand to haul myself the last couple of feet. The first question I meant to ask was, Where'd you find this beautiful solid piece of wood? But close up, I could see what it was: a door.

"From your house?" I gasped. No telling how he'd hauled it all the way uphill and wrestled it to the top of the tower.

He nodded. "Bedroom door. Suddenly popped in my head: aha!"

I crouched and ran my hands over the solid, paint-chipped surface. "It's *beautiful*. It's just—beautiful." My eyes were welling up again.

The emotion embarrassed him. "I hope you like."

"I love it. It's perfect. A perfect present." I would have jumped up and hugged him but for the feeling it would have embarrassed him even more. I did stand up, though, and turned around slowly, taking in the view. "Wow!" He grinned, shifting from one foot to the other. "And the flag—it's brilliant!"

He'd run a long piece of well pipe up through the hole where the doorknob had been and lined the top opening with rags so the flagpole set as snug as a flea. "We'll have to take better care of it from now on," I said. "You're not supposed to leave flags out in the rain and all that, but now we can roll it up and store it under the door—the platform, I mean. And we should protect the platform from all the cold and wet. Uncle Chet has an old canvas tarp he never uses—I'll haul it up for a cover."

"Good, good." He nodded.

"I can't get over it. It's so beautiful up here." And it was: the clouds had broken up after a rainy morning and now were clustered on the western horizon. Late-afternoon sunbeams shot through them, like a birthday present from God. I gave in to impulse then, grabbing Sogoji's hand and squeezing until his smile went a little twisty. "It's the best present I ever got. You're a genius, you know that?"

He looked down, blushing. "I am unworthy to—"

"Knock it off! That's Japanese talk, and you're an American just like me. This proves it—you've got real American can-do spirit. I've got to go, but meet me here Saturday afternoon at one sharp, okay?"

I was already on my way down the ladder. When I looked up, he was leaning over the edge of the platform with a big grin. "Okay!"

Daddy called that night to say for sure that he was getting off five whole days at Christmas and would be on the six forty-five train Friday evening, December 22. "I hear your class is putting on a Christmas program Saturday night," he said. "Can I come?"

"Sure—that'll be terrific!"

"Sounds like you're having a great birthday."

I told him it was the best ever—except for him not being there, of course. Besides the compass he sent, I got two brand-new Nancy Drew books from Estelle, a card with money from Grandma Anderson, and five dollars from Uncle Chet and Aunt Ruth. Mom gave me a trinket box with a ballerina inside.

She popped up and twirled to music when you opened the lid. I liked everything, but Sogoji's present was the one I thought about all evening and took to bed with me and woke up with in the morning. It was like the trinket box, only what popped up when I opened the lid was a glow of moonbeams.

I found a canvas tarp in the packing shed that more than covered the tower platform. In fact, there was enough to hang down one side, so on rainy days we could sit on the second level with the top platform overhead and a tent wall on one side. I borrowed some C-clamps to hold the canvas down and wah-la, as Margie would say: shelter.

Not only that, but when the flag was in place, I could see the top of it from our backyard—a perfect signal. Saturday at one was our regular meeting, but several times before Christmas, we met during the week: once he arrived first and set up the flag; the other times it was me. We made a sling to hang under the platform and that's where we stored the flag when we weren't on duty.

On Saturdays he brought the field glasses that used to belong to Jed, and the valley got the best looking-over it ever had. We spotted some planes, too, though when they flew directly overhead, Sogoji climbed down to the lower level so they wouldn't spot him. One of the planes flew so low the pilot saw me waving and wagged his wings in reply. With a little more height, I felt I could have touched them.

On rainy days—which was almost every day—we retreated

to the second-tier platform after surveillance. I brought an old kerosene lantern for light and a little warmth. We told stories and talked and read comic books when we didn't feel like talking. He'd never seen a comic up close before, and he fell absolutely in love with them. I let him borrow a few. Most of them belonged to Frank, but Sogoji took such good care of them, I could almost swear they came back in better condition than before.

Those were two of the best weeks of my life.

"But," I told him one afternoon, "we may not get to meet much over the holidays, with my dad here and the Christmas program and everything. Frank's coming a few days after Christmas, so I'll be busy during New Year's, too."

"That's okay. It's good you be with family. I can come up here by myself, keep a watch for you."

"Great. Remember—Jed's counting on us." Saying that, I had to believe that Jed had intended all along for us to be friends.

Sogoji nodded. "I know."

17

The Big Night

On the Friday before Christmas, Mr. Mayhew dismissed school at lunch recess so the decorating committee could get to work. Estelle got off at noon from the bank, but Mom's Citizens' League meeting lasted until three, which meant that once she got home, we were all rushing around like chickens to get the house in order and put a pot roast on to cook and bake an apple pie. By the time Uncle Chet's car pulled into the driveway with a beep of the horn, Mom was even more frazzled than usual: "Hazel, they're here—grab your shoes and a brush and come *on!*"

I ran out the front door barefooted, shoes and socks in hand, and all three of us piled into the backseat behind Uncle Chet and Aunt Ruth.

Now that the show was on the road, Mom calmed down, even though the jerks to my head as she brushed and braided my hair felt furious. After that job was done, she pulled on her gloves and straightened her hat and chatted brightly with Aunt Ruth about after-Christmas shopping. Aunt Ruth handed back the newspaper ads: Haughton's Ladies' Shop had just received a shipment of alpaca wool skirts from South America and the Shoebox was advertising a new selection of shoes.

"'Assorted styles,'" Estelle read from the newspaper. "I'll bet that means brown saddle oxfords or black saddle oxfords. What are the chances I can find a pair of black pumps?"

"You only have one shoe coupon until spring," Mom told her. "Get something sensible and go over your white pumps with black polish."

"Mother!" Exasperated, Estelle folded the newspaper. "Why not just go over my *feet* with black polish?"

We arrived at the station as the six forty-five train was pulling in with a squeal of brakes and swish of exhaust steam. By the time Daddy stepped off the center car with his leather suitcase in hand, we were all lined up on the platform. Mom started forward like the chairman of the welcoming committee, aiming to hand over the keys to the city. But instead, she collapsed in his arms and looked like she might cry before laugh-

ing. Estelle put an arm over my shoulders, holding me back.
"Isn't that sweet?"

I didn't answer. My braids still hurt. The minute Daddy
opened his arms to me, I was in them.

He was like the two aspirins a doctor told you to take before going to bed: everybody got calmer with him around. Mom
cooked breakfast in her nightgown next morning and played
hooky from the ration board meeting on Saturday afternoon.
She even laughed about the Christmas program—at least until
she had to start cooking for it.

It was weighing heavy on my mind, though. Not even the
beautiful taffeta dress (minus pinafore) hanging in the closet
could make me feel better about getting up in front of a room-
ful of people to present Mr. Mayhew with an award he didn't
even want. Mom was too busy to notice, but after lunch Daddy
called to me while I was on the way to my room. "Whoa, Nelly!
I'm headed out to the west orchard. Want to come?"

He didn't have to ask me twice. Before long we were walking under rattling apple branches while a cold mist strung beads
in my hair and wadded up the little gray clouds that puffed from
Daddy's pipe. A few yards down the row he stopped and pointed
his pipe stem at the base of a tree. "That looks like root fungus."
He frowned, adding, "I'd better tell Chet."

Whenever Daddy came home, he always noticed things
that Uncle Chet had missed. "Mr. Lanski could look at it," I
suggested.

He gave me a sideways glance. "Your mother says you've been spending a lot of time over there."

"Not a lot. But he doesn't have any help now that Jed's gone."

"He can hire all the help he needs; just too stubborn to admit he needs it. Your mother could use more help around here, though."

"Well . . ." I kicked at some fallen twigs that should have been raked up. By me, probably. "She's been awful bossy lately."

Daddy grinned. "What do you mean, 'lately'?" Then the grin disappeared, as though it knew it shouldn't be there. "The war's been as hard on her as it has on everybody else. I pray it won't last much longer, but in the meantime, we've all got to do our part—"

"I'm doing my part as hard as I can!" I burst out. After hearing this speech from Mom twice a week, I couldn't take it from him, too.

"Okay," he said after a minute. "What's the real problem?"

With no more encouragement than that, it all came out. Or most of it: the speech I had to give that night and how Mr. Mayhew might take it, my worries about Jed, my squirmy feelings about what was going on with Estelle. When I finished, we had reached the end of the row. Silently we turned the corner and had started up another row before Daddy took the pipe out of his mouth.

"I'll tell you what I've found out," he said. "The more you

stew over a problem, the worse it seems. But the stewed-over problems usually work out, and usually better than you expected.

"So let's take 'em one by one: I'll grant you, Estelle is kind of a flirt, but she's a sensible girl at heart, and if this thing between her and Jed is the real McCoy, she won't throw it away. And your teacher may get his nose a little out of joint at the program, but he'll get over it—real quick, most likely. Heck, everybody needs a pat on the back now and then. He may not let on, but I'll bet he feels a little glow inside when you say your piece. And as for that . . ." He paused as the house came in view, far away, framed by two rows of apple trees. "I'm not so keen on giving speeches myself. But here's what you do: look 'em all in the eye and think, 'I've got something real important to say to you people.' Then say it. You'll do fine."

The confidence in his voice made me feel better. But I also felt a little twinge at all that I hadn't told him, namely about my best friend—the "enemy." Sogoji was the most important secret I'd ever kept, exciting and a little scary at the same time. I was wondering if I shouldn't trust somebody with the secret—like Daddy—when he spoke up again.

"When something really bad happens, it takes us by surprise. The worst happens when you don't expect it. Why don't you run along home now—what do you want to bet your mother has something for you to do?"

That afternoon my mother ironed the green taffeta dress,

baked five dozen pigs-in-a-blanket using ten cans of hoarded Vienna sausages, stirred up four gallons of punch, and hemmed a new skirt for herself. Daddy was smart to stay out of the way. After I finished washing dishes, Mom ordered me into the bathtub. "And be sure to wash your hair—I need to cut your bangs before you get dressed. And remember we have to be there early so I can help set up the refreshment table."

After getting out of the bathtub and sitting still while Mom cut my bangs—too short, like she always did—I was dressed and buttoned and brushed up into a package that couldn't even be trusted on the front seat of the pickup between Daddy and Uncle Chet. "They'll muss up your dress," Mom said on her way out the door. "Put a blanket on the truck bed and sit back there with your skirt spread out." So I rode to school beside two jugs of sloshing punch, thinking it would serve my mother right if one of them tipped over on my dress and the truck pulled into the school yard with a big green Popsicle in back.

I couldn't sulk for long under that glittery sky, though. The clouds had lifted like a curtain on acres and acres of stars, some shivering, some quivering, some steady and unblinking as heavenly eyes.

But the schoolhouse took my breath away: the decorating angels had dropped by to drape paper chains and holly garlands from corner to corner. A nine-foot spruce stood at the front of the room, decked with tinsel and paper doves and ornaments made from tin cans. Some of the cans had holes punched in them to make designs. Without the candles inside, they just looked like holey cans, but the soft light transformed them. Even Marvin, the candle hater, was speechless. The tree made part of our stage set, which included a rocking chair and borrowed parlor furniture grouped around a cardboard fireplace, where Mr. Peters had set a lightbulb behind "flames" of colored cellophane.

Mr. Mayhew, in a suit so new it squeaked, stood at the door greeting parents and relatives as they arrived. Some weren't parents and relatives at all—when Mrs. Lanski waddled in on her husband's arm, I gasped in surprise. So did a lot of other people. She beckoned me over to her and put a heavy arm on my shoulders, whispering, "We heard so much about this program we just *had* to come." I thanked her, and meant it. While she greeted neighbors she hadn't seen since the picnic, the men scrambled to find a chair big enough for her. Over Mrs. Holmes's protest, they borrowed the parlor settee from the stage, since none of the actors would be sitting in it.

People kept coming until they filled the folding chairs and stood around the wall. To think of speaking in front of a crowd like this should have made me shake in my black patent shoes if they weren't so tight. But the night, the season, and the green taffeta were working some kind of magic. And not just on me— the entire class was quiet and ready at seven sharp, when Mr. Mayhew herded us to the front of the room and pretended to direct us in "A Midnight Clear" and "Silent Night." Even as

Mrs. Holmes did the real directing from the piano, there wasn't a snicker from Owen or a nudge from Marvin.

A pause followed the singing, while half the class returned to their seats in the front row. Marvin quietly slipped away and Margie wrapped herself in a shawl before taking her place in the rocking chair onstage. Mrs. Holmes left the piano and stepped forward to announce, "The class has written an original play to perform for you. It's called 'Watchman, Tell Us.' We hope you enjoy it."

Then she returned to the piano and gave a nod to Margie, who began with a big heavy sigh: "Here it is, Christmas Eve, and we haven't heard a word from Johnny—" (*Speak a little louder,* Mrs. Holmes signaled.) "IF HE WOULD JUST WALK IN THAT DOOR TONIGHT, IT WOULD BE THE BEST CHRISTMAS PRESENT OF MY LIFE."

Sherman entered with a load of wood for the fireplace. While setting it down, he dropped one log on his foot and made an exclamation that wasn't in the script. Margie frowned at him, and titters spread through the room. An audience of moms and dads will put up with all kinds of forgotten lines and missed cues. But when Susie came on, she stole the show with her cute faces—no one suspected she was such a ham. Margie didn't like it, and her lines started booming out like a drill sergeant instead of a sweet old mother longing for her son's return. Ivy and Owen made their entrances with food and presents, and the dialogue went over and over the sad fact that

Johnny couldn't be there. It was as boring as I expected, especially since they didn't include my suggestion for an air raid, or at least an air raid drill. I was nodding off when Margie stood suddenly, shouting, "LISTEN! WAS THAT A KNOCK AT THE DOOR?"

The outburst startled everybody, even the fidgety little kids and whining babies. For a second it was so quiet I could hear the tiny note blown from Mr. Edmund's pitch pipe. Then his unexpected voice boomed from the back of the room, singing: "Watchman, tell us of the night, what its signs of promise are."

Petilia stood up and sang, clear as silver on crystal: "Traveler, o'er yon mountain's height, see that glory beaming star."

As they exchanged lines back and forth, a stir began in the back of the room and worked its way forward. Marvin was limping down the center aisle, in a perfect imitation of Mr. Mayhew's walk. The olive-drab pants Sherman managed to borrow from his cousin were too tight around the waist, giving Marvin's face a look of patient suffering that suited his part. He arrived onstage at the end of the second verse, and family and friends gathered joyfully around. Owen pumped his hand furiously and exclaimed, "This whole country's proud of you, young feller. Thanks to you, the Stars and Stripes proudly wave over Guadalcanal." It was Owen's big line, and he couldn't help sneaking a glance at Mr. Mayhew. I did, too. The teacher's face was so pale his eyebrows stood out like dagger slashes.

Two chords banged from the piano and Jackie Erickson

poked me in the side. We were all supposed to stand up and face the audience as we sang the last stanza of the carol:

> *"Watchman, tell us of the night, for the morning seems to dawn.*
> *Traveler, darkness takes its flight, doubt and darkness are withdrawn.*
> *Watchman, let thy wanderings cease, hie thee to thy quiet home.*
> *Traveler, lo! The Prince of Peace, lo! The son of God is come!"*

Mrs. Holmes was nodding fiercely through rolling arpeggios, as though to say, Yes, children, that's *exactly* what I want. The final chords rang out with a flourish, and the notes melted away like frost.

Then the applause began, wild and heady. My stomach clenched up as I crossed over to the piano and picked up the slab of polished oak lying facedown on it. The applause faded as I turned to the audience.

Standing against the west wall, Daddy gave me the "okay" signal with his fingers. A flash caught my eye: the diamond ring on Mrs. Lanski's plump hand as she waved. My voice started out so high it didn't sound like anybody I knew: "In this season of peace and goodwill our thoughts turn to those who must think of war. . . ."

Behind me the class began humming "America the Beautiful" very softly. I stopped listening to myself and began listening to the moment. Everything fit, even Marvin's awful humming. When I asked Corporal Arthur Mayhew to come forward, he came, even though the eyes in his frozen face were so hot they could have burned holes. I offered him the plaque upside down, but he took it and even joined in the refrain as everyone stood: "America! America! God shed his grace on thee. . . ." By then there was hardly a dry eye in the house.

"I accept this award," said Mr. Mayhew, "on behalf of the many brave guys I left behind. They deserve all your thanks. For me, I'm satisfied with your warm welcome. It's going to be hard to leave, but at the end of the semester I expect to go back into active service—" Heads turned all over the room, especially the heads of school board members asking each other, Did you know about this? I saw my mother narrow her eyes and set her mouth: Re-enlist? We'll just see about *that*. I figured Mr. Mayhew didn't have a chance.

Afterward he clutched his plaque like a shield and shook every hand. The ladies were begging him to stay: "Just look what you did with these children tonight! You're a born teacher!" "My Owen has never been so excited about school!"

I felt a little sorry for him but mostly relieved that the ordeal was over and everybody seemed to think I'd done okay. Maybe better than okay: Mrs. Lanski was still dabbing at her eyes when I saw her after the program. "That was so moving, dear—the whole play, but especially your speech at the end. I couldn't help but tear up because—well, you know. . . ." That was the closest she'd ever come to admitting to me she had a boy in the service. I couldn't believe our dopey play had moved her so much, but the ending did turn out better than I'd thought. Mrs. Lanski was soon surrounded by sympathetic ladies who never gave her a chance to put the handkerchief away.

As for me, the praise, punch, and candlelight were so magical I missed sharing it with my best friend. And that gave me a wild idea.

18

A MIDNIGHT CLEAR

I squeezed into the back corner of the schoolroom, where all the desks had been pushed in a heap, and tore a sheet from my composition book. Some of the men, including Daddy, were catching up on local news nearby. I wasn't paying much attention until Mr. Peters said, "Yeah, and now thanks to the War Department, they'll be coming back from those camps. I think we should let 'em know right now that they won't be welcome here."

My ears perked up; what did the War Department do? Could the Japanese come back from camp now? How did I miss hearing about that?

"I don't know, Tom—" Daddy began.

"I do! We've been fighting Japs for three years now. Now all of a sudden the government opens those camps, and what are we supposed to do—kiss and make up like nothing ever happened? Erickson's dead against it. You know what the Japs did to his brother's boy in the Philippines."

Everybody knew how Mr. Erickson's nephew Sam had been treated so badly in a Japanese prisoner of war camp that he might not ever get over it. I nearly chewed up my pencil eraser, I was listening so hard. Mr. Schultz spoke up: "I hear there's a petition going around to pass a law saying the Japs can't come back—you mean to sign it, Tom?"

"Hell, yes—"

An angry voice broke in: "A lot of 'em are wearing American uniforms right now, fighting in Germany. What about them?"

The men started talking at once, but Daddy spoke over them. "Hey, fellows, it's Christmas. Peace and goodwill, remember?"

I tried to concentrate on my note. We needed a code—maybe after Christmas we could work on that. I drew a flag on a pole stuck in a pipe, which was our signal for meeting, then wrote 2-NITE and drew a clock with the hands at twelve. I folded the paper twice and scooted over to Mr. Lanski, who was standing by the door drinking punch out of a coffee cup.

"Good speech," he said.

"Thanks. Mr. Lanski, is it true the Japanese can come home from camp now?" He nodded. "What happened?"

"War Department decided they're not a threat, I guess."

"That's great! It means—"

He held up a hand to stop me saying too much. "We don't know what it means yet. They might not even want to come back."

Always looking on the bright side. Still, this was big news. I couldn't wait to talk it over with Sogoji. "Could you give this note to you-know-who? Right after you get home? And don't forget, please?"

He hesitated but then took the piece of paper and held it between two fingers. "Is this about something you shouldn't be doing?"

"Of course not!" At least, I didn't think so.

He frowned, even though that was his normal expression, more or less. "I caught him calling you on the phone the other day."

"But that was just—"

"Lookit," he said, in the kind of voice that didn't allow for argument. "I thought that taking him in was a fool idea from the start. Jed and the missus talked me into it, against my better judgment. But since we're in for the whole hog, I'm responsible for him. We're not out of the woods yet, so I'd feel better if you thought twice about anything that could get him in trouble." He wagged the note. "Is this anything that could get him in trouble?"

I thought twice and solemnly shook my head. But at the same time I decided we'd be more careful when planes flew over Hawk's Nest, at least for now.

"All right." Mr. Lanski slipped the message into his pocket. A while later, I saw him help his wife to her feet and out the door.

Our family was one of the last to leave, because of course my mom had to help clean up. Daddy pitched in, but even so it was nine o'clock before the job was done. For the ride home I sat up front—my dress being pretty well mussed by now. Mom squeezed in beside me because Aunt Ruth had already left in their sedan.

"How about that Lula Lanski?" Mom remarked once we were under way. "I'll bet that's the first time she's admitted in public that Jed was in the marines—it probably did her good."

"Maybe," Daddy replied. "But you remember what a drama queen she was in high school. She played more scenes than Greta Garbo." A few minutes later, when we turned onto the gravel drive leading to home, he said, "Hazel did a good job on her speech, didn't she?"

Mom struck her forehead with the flat of her hand. "Thanks for reminding me—I need to write a check to the engraver. Yes, Hazel, you did well. If the plaque hadn't been upside down . . ."

Mom was worn out, and Daddy followed her to bed right after the radio sign-off at ten. Estelle, who had come home earlier with Aunt Ruth, seemed restless. She sat on the sofa with her stationery box, but instead of starting a letter, she leafed through a magazine. Then she sewed buttons on a blouse, all the while sighing a lot. I had seen her slip out of the schoolhouse and happened to notice that Mr. Mayhew wasn't anywhere in sight at the time. But I didn't want to think about it, not tonight. At eleven, Estelle finished the blouse and went to bed. Soon everybody in the house—except me—was snoring away on cue.

I slipped out of bed and pulled my overalls up over a sweater, then grabbed my field glasses and a flat package I'd been keeping under my mattress. In the kitchen, I paused to put on my all-weather coat and slip a flashlight into the pocket before easing out the door, closing the screen very quietly behind me. Frank used to brag about sneaking out of the house after dark, but this was my first try.

Though it wasn't quite midnight yet, the sky sparkled with as many sides as a diamond, and every sound spoke like a voice. The very idea of Christmas—of silver bells and cut pine and peace on earth—was living and breathing in the air. The cold made me shiver, but it felt clean and healthy, not freezing and cruel. A sliver of a moon hung like a hunter's horn from a starry peg.

I followed the beam of my flashlight up to Hawk's Nest, humming "A Midnight Clear." At the top of the hill, the first thing I saw was a bed of coals, glowing like dragon's eggs on top of the tower. "Hey!" I called softly, and heard an answering reply.

Sogoji had brought the coals in an iron brazier, and their light gleamed off his white teeth when I climbed up.

"What a great idea!" I dropped down on my heels and stretched my hands toward the warmth. "How long have you been up here?"

"Not long. After the mister and missus go to sleep, I cleaned up the kitchen and took some coals from the wood-stove. This thing here—what do you call it?"

"It's a brazier."

"I found in the garage one time. Had to guess what it was for."

I laughed. "It's perfect for a campout! I've never camped out, have you?" He shook his head. "Frank used to go with the Scouts, but I never got a chance. Anyway, did you hear the news? About the Japanese being allowed to come back?"

He just nodded, without any expression I could make out.

"Well, aren't you excited?"

He looked down with a sideways glance and scraped a paint chip off the tarp with his thumbnail. His only answer to my question was a shrug. "Lula-san say you made a good speech."

"It was okay, I guess. Glad it's over." Deciding to drop the subject of camp for now, I tilted my head back and hugged my knees. "The stars look so big! Do you know any constellations? I just know the Big Dipper and Orion."

"She sang that song for me, about watchman and night. Said she's not heard it since she was little."

"Yeah, it's an old song."

"It made me think. You and me—watchmen in the night."

"I guess we are." I shivered. The coals warmed only one side of me, but the other side didn't exactly feel cold—it felt tingly.

"I bring tea. You want some?"

"You brought tea? Terrific!" He had brought more than that: out of a knapsack he pulled a thermos, two mugs, two cinnamon rolls, and two napkins, taking the idea of a midnight watch a lot further than I had. "I don't know why anybody ever thought you were dumb. You're smarter than any kid I know, to think ahead like you do."

His voice changed. "My father says—"

"Baloney!" Sogoji jerked in surprise, and I wondered if I'd stuck my foot in my mouth again. "Those cinnamon rolls smell good."

He took the hint and handed me one, wrapped in a napkin. "Not sweet enough," he said. "Sugar's low. I try to save for Christmas dinner, but Lula-san has sweet teeth."

"Tastes fine to me." It was warm, and the cinnamon smell stretched out lazily on the cold air. "Was Lula-san still crying when she got home?"

"Cry for what?"

"The play—it reminded her of Jed being away for Christmas."

"Huh. She said nothing about Jed, only about the other ladies and their talk and how she ought to get out more. And the food."

"Really? You think she'll start getting out more?"

He shrugged again, with a little smile. "She says lotta things she don't mean."

I remembered Daddy's comment about her tears and wondered if Mrs. Lanski wasn't facing up to reality even now. It made me uneasy, though I couldn't say why. I felt for the silver dollar through the pocket of my overalls. "Look at the moon. It would be tough to squeeze moonbeams for the empress out of a little sliver like that, wouldn't it?"

"They say a hare lives there."

"A what? You mean a rabbit?"

"A hare of many years with silver-white fur. He pounds rice to make rice cakes."

"Oh." I squinted at the moon, wondering who thought that one up.

"That star," he said, "in the song. Which is it?"

"You mean in the sky right now? None of 'em. That was a special star that only happened once. It showed where baby Jesus was so the wise men could find him in Bethlehem."

"Baby Jesus means the Prince of Peace, son of God is come?"

"Uh-huh." I took another sip of tea. "Everybody knows that." But then it struck me that "everybody" would only know that if they'd been told. "Do you know the Christmas story?"

"Not so good. Bits and pieces." That surprised me, but then, the Lanskis weren't big churchgoers. They might not even think to tell him unless he asked. "Tell me, please."

"Okay. Sure." I started slowly, then picked up steam: Mary and Joseph and the little town of Bethlehem, angels in the sky and shepherds in the field, wise men from the east following a star, wicked Herod slaughtering the babies of Judea. He listened so hard I could almost feel him listening, and wondered if the story sounded as fantastical to him as his stories sounded to me. But the details were so real—donkeys and oxen and a stable. In fact, it had never seemed so real to me before. "So when the wise men found the baby with Mary and Joseph, they took out the presents they'd brought: gold, and frankincense, and myrrh—that's some kind of perfume."

"Good story," he said after a moment.

"Thanks." That sounded funny; as if I had anything to do with it. "Hey—speaking of presents, I brought you one."

"Oh, Hazel. I have nothing for you—"

"Are you kidding? Your birthday present oughta do me until I'm fifteen. Anyway, this was all I could buy with my allowance. . . ." I handed over the package, wrapped in green paper. He carefully untied the ribbon, unwrapped the paper, and held the contents toward the light. "Comic books!"

"Uh-huh. 'Captain Easy: Mission to Berlin.'" Captain Easy wasn't my favorite, but he fought Germans, not Japanese.

"Thanks for most excellent gift!"

It didn't seem all that "excellent," compared to his. "Now you can start your very own collection."

"I will treasure them always." He carefully placed the three books in his knapsack. Then he glanced up, and the red glow of the coals flickered in his eyes. "Hazel!"

"What?"

"In yon sky—look, look! The star!"

I turned around to see where he was pointing, then caught my breath in amazement. A ball of reddish fire was pacing majestically among the stars, as though leading the way to—

"The Prince of Peace, the son of God is come!" Sogoji cried.

A noise like a thousand firecrackers boomed from the south and the light disappeared, quick as a hand snuffing a candle.

19

FIRE IN THE SKY

Of course after thinking about it, we both knew that the light in the sky wasn't the star of Bethlehem. But what was it? A Zero fighter plane blown out of the sky, like I'd always hoped to see? But there was no sound besides that firecracker boom. It could have been farther away than we thought, but still, an air fight was bound to be noisy all the way through, not just in the final explosion.

On Saturday morning I grabbed the newspaper after Daddy was through with it and pored over every page. To my amazement, not a word about a mysterious fire in the sky—

surely somebody had seen it besides us? At the top of the second page, though, I saw this:

STATEMENT TO RETURNING JAPANESE

It was set in a box signed by the American Legion, and began, "Under the War Department's recent ruling you will soon be permitted to return to this county." The next words slapped me in the face: "FOR YOUR OWN BEST INTERESTS, WE URGE YOU NOT TO RETURN. Certain incidents have already occurred that indicate the temper of the citizens of this county. . . ." The "statement" went on to promise help to any Japanese who wanted to sell their land, and a promise that the Legion would try to uphold law and order and "countenance no violence." That didn't make me feel any better, though, especially with the hint about "certain incidents." As I folded the newspaper, the smell of hot chocolate from the kitchen turned a little sour.

Christmas already seemed less merry because Frank couldn't be there. His work gang had voted to finish the armory in Gresham first so they could take a whole week off at New Year's before moving on to the next project. Estelle's mood dampened the big day even more. Mom was the one who planned the menu and the decorations and the carols, but Estelle usually made it all fun. Last year she woke everybody up on Christmas morning with "Welcome to Rio" playing on the phonograph as loud as it would go, pulled us out of bed, and led a conga line to the presents under the tree.

But this year I had to pry *her* out of bed and for the rest of the day she was edgy and tense. I knew for a fact that there was a soft squishy package wrapped in gold paper under her pillow. Late on Christmas night I got up to go to the bathroom and caught her having a phone conversation. "I've got to go now," she muttered into the receiver. "Bye." Then she explained to me, "I was just asking Mr. Hendricks when to be at work tomorrow."

Calling the bank president at 10:30 p.m. didn't seem likely, but I had my own problems. For three days I read every single headline in the newspaper, and none of them said anything about an explosion in the sky. It was hard to believe that no one else had noticed it—but if they hadn't, should I tell somebody? Like Daddy, for instance? He might think it was worth calling the FBI. But he might also ask, "And what were you doing on the hill at midnight anyway?" I could always say I'd spotted it from my window, but that was a flat-out lie and full of holes besides: how could I see anything in the southwest from a window that faced east?

I finally decided it wasn't worth the grief, especially with Frank coming in a few days. Frank could take the whole truth and nothing but, without giving me a third degree over my whereabouts at midnight. Better yet, Frank would know what to do. With that in mind, I didn't feel so gloomy seeing Daddy off at the train station a couple of days after Christmas.

The very next day, a noisy van clattered into Ash Grove. It wasn't exactly Charles Atlas who jumped out of the back door, but neither was it the old pale Frank whose Scout uniform bulged a little in the middle when he was in it. He had turned sixteen while away and looked every bit of it: brown and fit, slimmed-down and bulked-up and a whole inch taller. Mom's face went through half a dozen expressions before he reached her, picked her up, and swung her around in a circle. Then she laughed, beating his shoulder with one fist. "Put me down, you big galoot!"

I got a soft punch on the jaw and a "How's it goin', kid?" It wasn't a good start.

For the rest of the day my mother—and Estelle, too, when she got home from work—insisted on treating him like a returning hero, even though all he'd been fighting was lumber and pipe. All day it was, "Would you like some hot chocolate, Frank?" and "I'm making ham patties and green beans tonight—your favorite!" and "How about another piece of lemon cake before I put it away?"

The next morning he asked for cackleberries and gaskets, meaning eggs and pancakes, knowing that we never got both. But Mom just laughed and said he'd learned a new language while he was away. After breakfast he told her she was the best egg buster in the business and he was off to visit the feather merchants but would be back in time for blanket detail and chow that night.

After a few days I felt like smothering him with a pillow. He wouldn't let me tag along to see his feather merchant pals (meaning "civilians"), but I guessed he spent the time swapping lies and listening to dance records and saying, "What's the score?" and "You dig me?" To me he just said things like, "What's up, kid?" and never waited for an answer. Once he even patted me on the head, like I was a puppy. Whenever I tried to start a conversation, he always had something better to do.

It all came to a head on New Year's Eve. Our family tradition was to gather at Uncle Chet's for popcorn and hot cider, play Monopoly and gin rummy, and burn the Christmas tree in the big fireplace while counting down until midnight. But without telling anyone, Frank and Estelle had made other plans. Frank was going to a party given by one of his buddies in Odell. Mom was already upset with him after she'd found a couple of half-smoked cigarettes (which he called "captain's butts") in his room. But this was the last straw: "You haven't spent more than thirty minutes with your own family, and you *know* what we always do on New Year's Eve. . . ."

To Estelle, Mom didn't say anything, just went about her chores with tight lips and narrowed eyes. That's because Estelle was going to a dance in Hood River—with Mr. Mayhew. I wasn't so quiet about it, especially that night, when I ran back from Uncle Chet's house to get some oranges and caught Estelle in the bedroom pulling on a pair of nylon stockings. "Where'd you get those?"

She couldn't quite meet my eyes. "None of your beeswax."

"So that's what was in the gold package under your pillow! You thought you could sneak out of the house without us noticing. How did 'Artie' get them for you? On the black market?"

"I don't—come on, Hazel . . . I don't deserve this—"

It was the last straw for me. I turned my back on her and marched to the living room, where I flipped through our record rack to find the Andrews Sisters. Next minute, Patty, Maxene, and LaVerne were belting out, "Don't sit under the apple tree, with anyone else but me—"

Estelle charged out of the bedroom and plucked the needle off the record, making an ugly scratching sound. "Look. It's not like Jed and I are *officially* engaged."

"I'll bet he thinks you are. And I'll bet he wonders why your letters are so short. That's no way to treat a fighting man!"

"Artie's a fighting man, too! If you only knew what he's been through. He could sit out the rest of the war with his bad leg, but he decided to re-enlist. Helping him have a good time before he goes back is the least I can do."

"And taking stockings from him is the next least you can do."

"Oh—you—" Unable to say exactly what I was, Estelle whipped the record off the phonograph and broke it over her knee.

I was already furious, but this made me even more furious.

"What—! What are you—! I'm going to write a letter to LaVerne Andrews and tell her what you did!"

"Oh, Hazel, stop being so silly." Which was fine for her to say, standing there with two pieces of broken record in her hands. Her face was as red as mine felt. It was the kind of argument we'd probably both be sorry for tomorrow, but I didn't care.

"You'll regret this," I said.

She tried to laugh. "You sound like a movie."

Needless to say, 1945 came in without a whole lot of cheer.

Estelle managed to be home by the twelve-thirty curfew that night, but Frank dragged in at an hour past. He got a lecture at 1:30 a.m. and another at ten when Mom finally rousted him out of bed. "If you can do work projects for your country, you can do a little work for us, too. Your uncle Chet is burning brush this afternoon and he expects you to join him."

For once, I appreciated my mother's drill-sergeant act. It took some of the starch out of Frank: after an afternoon of piling brush he was halfway back to being human. When the dishes were done and Mom and Estelle were listening to Jack Benny on the radio, I came to the door of his pantry bedroom. "I have to talk to you."

Sprawled out like that, he looked twice as big as Sogoji. He glanced up, shrugged, and nudged over the pile of comic books at the foot of the bed. I perched on the corner and got right to the point. "While you were away, I've been using your field glasses to go up to Hawk's Nest—"

He rolled his eyes. "So you've kept the HRJAAP going all by your lonesome?"

"Whenever I get a chance. And I keep a logbook just like you used to. It hasn't always been easy, but—"

"But you've done your part in the fine old Anderson tradition. I'm proud of you, Nut."

He turned a page as I choked down my first response. "Just *listen* a minute. I might have seen something, and I wanted to ask what you thought. It was on the night before Christmas Eve. . . ."

As I talked, a change came over him. He didn't seem to pay much attention at first, but then his eyes stopped moving across the page, and next they weren't on the page at all, and finally they were staring right at me, round and amazed.

"Where'd you see this thing? Which direction?"

"Southwest, I think—toward Mount Hood. Not many people live back there, so maybe nobody saw it. The paper never had anything about it."

"Did it blink, or was it more like a fire that doesn't burn very long?"

"Like a fire, kind of red. So—"

I almost said, "Sogoji saw it first," but stopped just in time. After a swallow, I went on, "The light only lasted a few seconds.

It was moving, but there was no engine noise at all, just a big boom. So I know it wasn't a plane."

Frank closed the book and laid it down. "I'm going to tell you something in strict confidence, you dig?"

I nodded, unblinking.

"A couple of weeks ago the boss told our team leaders to be on the lookout for lights in the sky, day or night."

"What kind of lights?"

"Don't know. They didn't say."

"What are you supposed to do when you see one?"

"Tell the boss."

"And who does he tell?"

"They didn't say."

"What do you think it is?"

For a minute Frank looked like an eager Boy Scout again. "I think the Japs are up to something. We'd better go have a look."

20

The Tuesday Patrol

This was more like it, I thought. It was good to know that some things didn't change: under the new Frank who gabbed about jamming with the fellows, there was still an old Frank who had studied Japanese in order to know his enemy and spent hours on a hill looking for foreign planes.

He told Mom that he'd promised to go hiking with me, and Mom thought he was sweet to make time for his little sister. As the two of us set out early Tuesday morning with our provisions, she called, "Be careful—stay on the trails and be back before dark."

Dark came early these days, so we couldn't waste any time. Frank had already mapped out a route. "We'll head southwest along the logging road and try to get all the way to the lake if the snow doesn't stop us. That'll give us some elevation. We'll stop for chow at the old Scout camp and look around. If we don't see anything, we'll go north and come back along the lava beds. That's a lot of territory."

Once we got under way, we didn't say much. Frank seemed to be wrapped up in his own thoughts, so to help pass the time, I imagined myself setting off with one of Jed's fellow marines. A cold fog iced the ground, so I had to stretch my imagination pretty hard to get back to the jungle. We were checking out a radio message that the FJC and I had picked up. The details were unclear, but I was pretty sure the Japs were building a communications post on the island. "It's amazing how you picked up on Japanese so fast," the marine told me. "I've studied it myself, and it's a tough language." I just smiled and put a finger to my lips.

"Not very chatty today, are you?" Frank remarked over his shoulder. "Did you pack any of that lemon cake?"

Southwest led us directly toward Mount Hood, with its long steep slopes and patches of deep forest. Within half an hour I was sweating and Frank had tied his government-issue jacket around his waist. His manly stride took him so far ahead I had to yell at him every now and then to wait up. For that I got called a slowpoke, but by the time we reached the lake, he was panting, too. We'd covered four miles in three hours, most of it uphill and the last half mile through six inches of snow.

The waters of Middle Fork rattled over a rocky bed near the lake, which was covered by a skin of ice. Frank found the old Scout campground and cleared a place in the snow. We started a fire with our kindling and matches and built it up with windfall branches.

When the fire burned down to cooking coals, Frank made a circle of rocks for a camp stove and dumped a can of tomato soup into the skillet. "Some fun, hey, Nut?" His good humor was thawing out.

"Uh-huh." I was wondering if Sogoji and I could come up here sometime. Probably too risky, but I could see us sipping tea over his cast-iron brazier and telling each other stories. "You want a cheese sandwich?"

By the time we finished our sandwiches, the soup was hot. I poured a mug for him. "Frank?" He grunted to show he was listening. "What do you think of the Japanese?"

"What's to think? They're the enemy."

"I mean, the American ones, like the Miasako brothers. They were okay, weren't they?"

"They were Japs. Everybody knows Japs are sneaky. They smile and bow and act so polite, then they turn around and stab you in the back. Tom and Lew seemed like regular guys. But after Pearl they started getting on my nerves. So patriotic all of a sudden—when we said the pledge, you could hear them over everybody else."

I remembered that time he came home from school with a black eye and swollen cheek. "Is that why you got in a fight with them?"

He blew on his cup and a puff of steam clouded his face. "Sort of. They had a shortwave radio—Lew bragged about how they'd worked all summer to buy it. I went over to their house after school one time to listen to the news from Europe. It was swell. But after Pearl they clammed up about it, and Claude Roberts got suspicious. He talked it over with some of us guys, and we formed a committee to ask them to give up the radio."

"A committee?" Sounded like a gang to me.

"Sure, like the Citizens' League. We asked them— politely—to turn over the radio so everything would be clear and aboveboard. And they wouldn't do it. So that only made us more suspicious, natch."

After a long silence, I had to prompt him. "And then . . . ?"

"Well, we didn't have any choice. Persuasion didn't work, so we had to use force."

"How?"

"We jumped 'em on their way home from school. They were warned, and a few of their Jap pals came along for protection, so it was some fight. But we won. Claude promised them more of the same unless they turned over the goods. So they did."

"But . . . Wasn't that stealing?"

"C'mon, Nut. The government ended up confiscating all their radios anyway."

"Did Claude turn it in?"

"Sure! Of course we used it for a few weeks, to make sure it was in good shape. Why are you so worried about the Japs?"

"Well . . . With the camps opening up, they'll be coming home soon. Hadn't we better worry about them?"

"Don't be so sure they'll be coming back."

"What do you mean?"

"They might get the idea they're not welcome here."

"But that's not fair! It wasn't fair in the first place, to pack them all off to camps when they hadn't done anything."

Frank rapped his head with his knuckles. "Use your nut, Nut. They may have lived here for thirty years, but they're *still Japanese.* The older ones don't even speak English, hardly. Suppose the shoe was on the other foot and you were an American living in Japan, running a factory or teaching English. You learn to get along with the people so you can do business—you might even like some of 'em. But when the bombs start to fall, whose side are you going to be on? Your Jap friends' or your own folks'?"

I tried to imagine myself in Sogoji's split-soled shoes. "But a lot of them were born here; they've never even seen Japan. We've got Japanese soldiers in our army. Don't they *want* to be Americans?"

Frank slurped up the last of his soup. "Once the war's over, we'll sort out the loyal Japs from the other kind." He stood, brushing off his pants. "I think we should've waited till then to open the camps, but nobody asked me."

"When Tom and Lew come back—I mean, if they do—will you go back to being friends with them?"

Frank snorted, fed up with the conversation. "What would we have to be friends *about*?" He bent over to pick up his field glasses. "I'm going up the cliff to have a look."

That meant leaving me to clean up the camp, but he was gone before I could yell about it. I scattered the coals with a stick and rubbed the mugs with snow to clean them, then stowed away the rest of the food and went looking for Frank. I found him on a flat rock that jutted over the east end of the lake. "Thanks for sticking me with the cleanup detail!"

"Slab your crabbing and come over here. Careful—it's slippery." He had his binoculars turned on a spot directly north. "There's a white speck down there. Just about where the lava bed starts, on the left. See it?"

After a little wobbling around with the field glasses, I saw what he was talking about. The lava bed, left over from the mountain's days as an angry volcano, lay like a big gray scab on the woody slope. Following it from near end to far, I located the white speck. In the binoculars it looked like a sheet thrown over some bushes to dry. "Can we get down there?"

"I think so. But it'll take at least an hour. I'll take the coordinates and we'll get on our way as soon as we can, okay?"

Half an hour after we set off from the lake, I was panting to keep up again. No doubt about it: the Young America Corps had made Frank tougher and stronger. But I wasn't sure it made him better. Even though he'd grown an inch, I wasn't looking up to him like I used to. How could he go along with a bully like Claude Roberts and take something the Miasakos had worked so hard for? I was sure I'd never do anything like that.

We followed Middle Fork for a quarter mile, then struck out along the hiking trails. They weren't so bad—though overgrown, at least they were trails. But for the last leg of our journey there was no path at all: just Frank's compass showing the way across wilderness, with gravel slides and windfalls that the compass never knew of. When we finally reached the tip of the lava bed, almost two hours after setting out from the lake, both of us felt pretty battered. The frozen rock was rippled up like corrugated cardboard and slick with ice. We nearly crashed a dozen times while making our way across it, but finally our objective came in view, tucked in a thicket of juniper.

Tangled and ripped, it still looked like a big sheet thrown out to dry. Or else just thrown out. "Maybe a parachute!" Frank said, lunging forward.

I hung back. "If it is . . . do you think there might be a parachutist somewhere? Alive or . . . dead?"

Frank looked back at me, suddenly pale. Then he licked his lips. "Come on."

The white thing swelled in the wind, then flattened, like it was taking its last breath. Coming closer, we could see that the corners and edges were charred black, and black scraps fluttered in the bushes all around. Frank touched the white material carefully, rubbing it between his fingers. "I can't figure out what this stuff is."

I inched closer and ran my fingers over the surface. It wrinkled in sharp waxy lines, like the accordion folds of a Chinese lantern. I took two handfuls and tugged. "It doesn't tear easy."

"But look at this." Frank had found a seam where two layers of the peculiar material overlapped. "The pieces are glued together. If it was silk or nylon, they'd be sewn." He opened his pocketknife and made a cut. "See? No threads. It's almost like some kind of paper."

I traced the seam with my fingers, following it along a curve toward the place where other seams appeared to join up.

"You know what this looks like?" Frank asked excitedly. "It's almost like a hot-air balloon. See how it's rounded over here— and there's some wire rigging! It's attached to . . . Hold on. . . ."

He crept away from me through the brush, pulling a long strand of wire free from the scrub. I found a piece of wire, too, and started pulling from the other end.

"Hold on, I think I found something!" Frank was almost gasping as he worked his way toward the end of the line. "It looks kind of like . . . like a . . ."

Suddenly his voice clanged like a fire bell as he lunged toward me, screaming, "Hazel! Get *down*!"

He made a leap, and we hit the ground together. Juniper branches angrily clawed at us, gouging at my mouth and eyes. Next thing I knew, my head was tucked against Frank's chest with both his arms wrapped around it. "What's the matter?" I wailed into his jacket.

"Hold still! It's a bomb!"

My mind went absolutely blank. Only it was a big, booming blankness that forced out all sound. It seemed to last a long time but couldn't have been more than a few seconds before I started hearing things again—the icy trickle of water in a faraway creek bed, the breeze humming through juniper branches, and Frank whispering as though he were in church—except the words wouldn't do for church.

He released his grip on me and sat up. Then he stood, carefully. I did, too, and when he took a couple of steps in the direction he'd come from, I followed. "No closer!" he warned. "Look."

He was pointing at a tangle of burned wires and lumpy metal in the juniper bushes. There was an object nestled in the branches, lying at a tilt. It was about two feet long, bullet-nosed at one end and fin-tailed at the other. It looked like a torpedo: the kind shown in newsreels, jiggling down the assembly line in some munitions factory.

"Dirty, stinking bastards," Frank said bitterly. "They could have blown us both up."

"Who?" My voice sounded like it had been stomped on.

"The *Japs*. Who else?" He pointed to some markings I hadn't noticed before, half hidden by the folds of the parachute—or balloon, or whatever it was. My eyes fixed on them like magnets, and my brain seemed to slide back to that moment three months ago when I came across another piece of paper tangled in the brush. Japanese writing on that one, too. Here was a great big piece of paper, with bigger marks, and at that moment it seemed that one had led to the other as sure as night follows day. Feeling dizzy, I dropped to my knees.

Frank sounded furious, but not at me. "God only knows why it didn't go off. I don't dare touch anything. We'd better get away from here and go straight to Uncle Chet's, 'cause he's closest. And then we call the FBI. I've got the number somewhere."

For the first time I noticed his voice shaking, but my whole body was shaking, so I couldn't fault him for that. We backed away from the debris, adjusted our knapsacks, and set off across the tumbled rock as fast as our wobbly legs could go.

21

THE YANKS ARE COMING

The day's journey had taken us in a big loop: south of the orchard first, then west and north. All we had to do to get home was cut across the top of the loop, but that took over an hour through rough country. By the time we got to Uncle Chet's, scratched-up and breathless, it was almost dark. Aunt Ruth called Mom as soon as she heard our story. Mom came right away with Estelle, and what with the women exclaiming, "You could have been killed!" over and over, and searching for phone numbers and finding someone at the FBI office in Portland who would listen to us, it was quite a night.

When we finally got home, the rest of the evening felt like a warm bath in Epsom salts, with extra hugs and kisses and a phone call from Daddy thrown in: "Are you all right, Hazel?" he asked. "You sound like you're taking it well. I'm proud of you, sweetheart. And I'm really grateful—" His voice choked off then, and he asked to speak to Mom again. It all would have been wonderful, except that I couldn't feel anything. It was like an evil witch had crept in and turned me to stone.

At bedtime, which was past eleven that night, I slid between the cold sheets thinking that my brain was about to turn off like a radio. But sleep didn't come. Instead my mind kept flashing with the light from an exploding bomb that could have been the last thing I ever saw.

They could have blown us both up, Frank said . . . blown us up. An ocean away, some small, squinty-eyed people I didn't even know had made a plan to send a bomb my way, knowing it could kill somebody. Kill *me*! Dirty, stinking Japs . . .

At seven-thirty next morning, Frank was in the bedroom shaking me by the shoulder. "Get up, Nut. There's a captain from army intelligence and two G-men from the FBI in the living room. They want to ask us some questions. Hurry!"

Captain Sanders was nice. He talked to me like he might have had a twelve-year-old girl of his own once, but the other two acted like they had never seen a twelve-year-old girl in their lives. That may have been why they let the captain do most of the talking. He pulled a kitchen chair up to the sofa where Frank and I sat side by side. The G-men occupied the two armchairs and Mom hovered in the background while Estelle rattled around in the kitchen making coffee. "Now," Captain Sanders said, after the introductions were over. "Just to get the story straight: let's hear what you two saw yesterday. You go first, Frank, and then we'll hear from Hazel."

Frank began with our setting out in the icy morning—hard to believe it was only yesterday—and told the story so plainly and thoroughly I couldn't see anything to add to it. But when Frank got to the end he said, "There's one more thing we should tell you, sir."

"What's that, son?"

"The reason we went up there in the first place. Hazel told me that two nights before Christmas she was outside, on a hill near our house, and saw something like a fireball in the sky."

The room seemed to shift as everyone stared at me. I felt like I'd suddenly been stripped down to my underwear. Then the questions started: Outside? Where? When? Can you describe the light you saw? How big? How long?

I held up pretty well until one of the FBI agents leaned forward and demanded, "What possessed you to be out there in the first place?"

Even though in my imagination I'd always faced up steely-eyed to Japanese interrogators and enemy firing lines, I felt my lip quiver and my voice give way. It wasn't just the G-man; maybe it wasn't him at all. The brightness of those stars came back to me and how warm I'd felt in spite of the cold. And all that time, there was a bomb floating in the midnight sky. With a shift in the wind it could have drifted lower and closer and blown me to pieces, even while I was telling the Christmas story. . . .

The captain noticed how I felt but misunderstood why. "Hold up on the grilling, Inspector. I think all of us remember sneaking out at night. It doesn't take a lot of explanation for anybody with an ounce of gumption, right, Hazel?"

That did it; after holding up like a little soldier since yesterday, I burst into tears. Mom swooped down beside me and the interview bumped to a close. The men had the information they wanted anyway, so when Captain Sanders's efforts to calm me didn't help, they began gathering up coats and hats.

"One more thing before we go," the captain said. "Frank, we really appreciate the information you and your sister gave us, but it must stop here. The U.S. government is on the case. We'll get it cleared up, but the last thing anybody needs is for wild rumors to break out and start a panic. So I'll have to ask all of you, as a patriotic duty, not to say anything about what you saw. That's an order."

"Just a minute, sir." Frank stepped into the captain's path. "Just one thing I'd like to know. Was that a live bomb? Could it have gone off if we'd tripped over it or anything?"

Captain Sanders, cap in hand, glanced around the room. "We're taking care of it, son. No need to worry."

"I'm not worried, sir; I'd just like to know."

"Sure. Of course you would. But there are some things we can't tell. You understand that, don't you, Frank?"

With that, he clapped Frank on the shoulder, turned down Estelle's offer of a cup of coffee, and followed the G-men out the door. Mom patted my shoulder until I stopped sniffling. Then she stood up, briskly smoothing her apron. "Well, we got our marching orders, didn't we? Let's eat breakfast so Estelle can get to work and Hazel to school. Frank, Aunt Ruth will be here at nine-thirty. You need to be ready."

"Ready for what?"

"Remember? You promised to give a talk about Young America Corps to the Citizens' League this morning."

"The Citizens' League?" Frank half shouted. "With enemy bombs being floated at us from Japan?"

"Oh, Frank, how could that be? All the way across the Pacific in *balloons*?"

"Where'd they come from, then? Germany? Who else are we at war with?"

"I don't know what's going on, but you heard the captain— they're looking into it. Now we have to practice keeping our lips zipped."

Frank snorted. "They oughta tell us what's up. There's probably more bombs where that one came from. And they're not aimed at battleships or military bases—*any*body could stumble on one."

"That's true, Mom." Estelle stood at one end of the sofa with a cup of coffee. "But they couldn't have come all the way from Japan. What if they were launched from enemy ships and the government is just not telling us?"

"Right!" Frank said. "Or a secret weapons plant! There could be spies up in the mountains! They could have a signal tower!"

The words *signal tower* struck me like lightning.

Mom pressed her lips together in a thin straight line while she took a breath. "As the captain said, they're working on it. There's no point in us making ourselves sick with worry over something we can't help. You and Hazel have done what you could. Now we can go on about our business and let the army do theirs."

I no sooner got my breakfast down than it came up again. That led to my temperature being taken and some head shaking and tongue clucking from Mom, who finally put me to bed with a hot-water bottle.

Estelle left for work, and a while later Aunt Ruth pulled up in the car. Frank was still complaining as he went out the door.

I lay in bed, eyes wide open. Even with a hot-water bottle, I couldn't stop shaking.

Signal tower . . . signal tower . . . We'd built one, hadn't we? I wanted it for observation, but what did *he* want it for? I remembered what he told me before Christmas: "I can come up here by myself, keep a watch for you." But maybe he had another purpose in mind all along. It was his idea to build a flagpole and use it for a signal—what if he wanted to signal someone besides me? Who could say for sure he wasn't in contact with an enemy relay station, right under our very noses?

Of course, any bomb that hit me that night would have blown him up, too. But what did that matter to somebody who defended kamikaze pilots and believed that suicide was honorable? I began putting together things he'd said, and how he'd gone out of his way to meet me and win me over, and how eager he was to help me build the tower. Japs were sneaky. . . . But was *he* one of *them*? Even while pretending to be my friend?

Frank said it: What have we got to be friends *about*?

The ticking of the clock in the empty house was starting to drive me batty, so I threw back the covers, went to the kitchen, and turned on the radio, just in time to catch the ten o'clock news. I ran a glass of water from the tap and gulped it down as the announcer said, ". . . beating back the German offensive in France. In the Pacific, Japanese forces are on the run in the Philippines as American forces continue their advance. Marines have landed on Mindoro and secured the base for an assault on Luzon. Heavy casualties have been reported at Mindoro, but General MacArthur confidently expects success. . . ."

Radio announcers always played up the good news. Even bad news, like "heavy casualties have been reported," usually mentioned somebody expecting success. How much were they not telling us? What if there were more balloons in the sky right now, floating death over our heads?

I ran to my room and hurried into my overalls, slipping Jed's silver dollar into my pocket just before grabbing the field glasses.

The air was so still that my breath fell behind me as I ran across the yard and into the woods. After reaching Hawk's Nest, I headed straight for the tower and climbed to the top, panting.

The view from up there still took me by surprise—with just a little more height, I could imagine seeing all the way to the Pacific. If somebody had a signal lantern, how far would it reach? I turned the field glasses on Mount Hood, looking for any sort of structure or smoke—or any speck of white, in the sky or on the ground. Slowly moving west, I spotted the lake and Middle Fork and could have made out our campground from yesterday if there weren't so many trees in the way. Next I looked for the lava bed—and clamped my jaw to keep from yelling out loud.

Two jeeps were parked in a clearing just north of the bed. As I watched, a military truck pulled up and men swarmed out from under the tarp. Some were in uniform, some not, but they all carried rifles. They formed a rough circle around a fellow with a peaked officer's cap who might have been Captain Sanders. He was pointing in different directions, and everywhere he pointed, two or three men peeled off. I guessed their mission: to search for signs of bombs, balloons, or anything Japanese. Anything at all. I bit my lip so hard it hurt.

Then a roar like twenty buses charging uphill without mufflers made me swing the glasses eastward. Through spaces in the evergreens I made out the flat, olive-drab tops of a convoy of military vans, all headed up Highway 35. Scarcely breathing, I watched two of them turn off in my direction. The Yanks were coming! There could only be one reason—they meant to search the whole valley, working their way through the fields and orchards and over to this very hill!

22

THE RIGHT THING

The glasses thudded against my chest. One of the search parties was sure to find an abandoned house by the creek, and with that shrine in the bedroom it didn't look so abandoned. That would lead them to the Lanskis' house, and if somebody happened to catch sight of a black head through the kitchen window, they'd surround the place with their rifles leveled—

Let 'em! I thought. Let 'em round up all the dirty, stinking Japs in the neighborhood!

My heart was thumping hard enough for two people. In fact, I *was* two people. One of them had just been through the shock of her life, discovering what the enemy could do. The other . . .

The other had one friend who happened to look like the enemy. My whole chest hurt, like the two of them were inside, slugging it out.

From somewhere down below, a truck motor belched as it downshifted for a steep climb. I opened my mouth and a gulp of cold air rushed in. It seemed to blow me back into myself.

Next minute, I was scrambling down the other side of the hill, stumbling over fallen logs and whippy saplings. By the time I reached the Lanskis' front door, I felt time driving me like a demon.

Mr. Lanski answered my knock. For a split second he looked glad to see me. "Where's the fire? You've got a scratch on your cheek."

I brushed the back of my hand across my face and it came away with a smear of blood. "Mr. Lanski—Sogoji had better hide. Here's what happened—"

I told the whole story, knowing he wouldn't go and start any wild rumors. While I talked, he stepped out on the porch and closed the door behind him. In a flash, I remembered when he'd done that before: almost three years ago, when Frank and I had come over to ask his permission to use the hill. Funny to think that he was protecting Sogoji then, just as he was now. Well, we both were. ". . . So you'd better go clear out the old house," I finished. "And keep him out of sight. I don't know how long they'll be on the lookout."

"I will. Thanks, Hazel." That might have been the first time he'd ever called me by name. "You got time to step in for a minute?"

I was already backing away. "No. I don't have time—and you don't, either. There's a truck headed this way right now. Hurry!"

I turned around and took off before he could say more. It's true that there was no time. But something else was true, too: I didn't want to see Sogoji. I was almost afraid to see him, as though the sight of him would make the word *Jap!* go off like a fire alarm. Less than twenty-four hours ago I'd been scared out of my wits by a bomb. I'd just been scared back into them—but barely.

When I got back home, I washed my face and put an ice cube on the scratch to make it stop bleeding. Then I flopped on the bed, overalls and all, and took a lot of long, slow breaths until my heart settled down. The clock in the living room ticked louder and louder, every tick asking, Did you do the right thing? Did you? Did you?

Yes, yes, yes, *yes*. Sogoji was Japanese. But he wasn't a Jap.

When I got to school on Thursday, the whole class was buzzing. For one thing, Mr. Mayhew had finally given an interview to

Sherman's brother for the newspaper, and the article was due to appear that very day.

But the military sweep of the neighborhood had caused an even bigger buzz. It was being called a "routine operation," but everybody knew there was nothing routine about a bunch of soldiers and civilian patrol searching backyards. The minute I walked in the schoolhouse door, I was surrounded. "I hear you and your brother found part of a Jap plane in the woods," Owen charged. "Is that true?"

My pulse was pounding in my ears. "I'm not allowed to say anything about it."

"What do you mean, not allowed?"

"Captain Sanders of U.S. Army Intelligence told me not to say anything about it." It helped to remember Terry Lee being interrogated by the Dragon Lady; I set my face the same stern way.

"No kidding? Wow." Owen stepped back, as though to allow me more space. "So you really did find . . . What did you find?"

"I can't tell you—"

"Okay, okay." By this time the whole student body was listening in and I felt their respect growing like a bubble around me. I wasn't sure I liked it.

Mr. Mayhew was late that day, as if his decision to re-enlist meant that he could coast to the end of semester. But the end of semester was still two weeks away, and the afternoon stretched long and empty. He was desperate enough to ask for suggestions about what to do. Margie suggested a preview of the newspaper article, and Roger wanted to clear the floor for a wrestling competition, but neither won. Mr. Mayhew announced he would start reading *Tom Sawyer* the next day, and dismissed school early.

The minute I got home, I changed clothes and reached for the field glasses. But they weren't on the bedpost.

"I packed 'em," Frank said when I ran to his room. "They're at the bottom of my duffel bag." He was due to "ship out"—as he put it—the next day for a work project at Bonneville Dam.

"But I need them!" I wailed.

"What for? They belong to me, you know. With Jap bombs floating around I'll have to keep a lookout. That's a pretty high priority."

I plunked down on his bed and bit my lip. My priority seemed just as high as his, but he had the argument sewn up. I should have asked for my own field glasses for Christmas instead of a Swiss army knife. "The U.S. Army is keeping a lookout," I said weakly.

"Maybe. But I don't get it, Nut. We had one visit from army intelligence and one sweep through the neighborhood and now it's like nothing happened. Or like they're *pretending* nothing happened."

"The kids at school know we found something. Did you tell anybody?"

"Well." He picked up a stack of comic books and tried to stuff them in the top of his duffel bag. "One of the guys asked me if I knew anything, and I sorta told him I did."

"You *sorta* told him! The captain said we weren't to tell anybody anything!"

"I didn't say *what* I knew. Only that I knew *some*thing. And anyway." He gave up on the comic books and slapped them down on the bedspread. "There's bound to be more bombs out there. The army's keeping it quiet for their own reasons—sure, they don't want people to panic, but I'll bet they also don't want the Japs to know their bombs actually got here. But suppose some kids are hiking around and stumble over a live one, because they were never told to be on the lookout?"

"It wasn't a live bomb we found. Or else it would have exploded in the fire that burned the parachute, wouldn't it?"

He hesitated, then lowered his voice. "Here's what I think: the bomb we found was in the same payload as the one that exploded that night over the hill."

"But—"

"That balloon was carrying at least two bombs. Maybe more. Just one was enough firepower to blow you to smithereens if it had drifted a little closer. What we found was probably a dud. But one of these days, somebody might stumble over a live one."

Frank jerked the cord on his duffel bag and tied it shut.

"Bombing innocent civilians—*that's* what Japs are like. You see now why we had to lock them up?"

Not all of them are like that, I thought stubbornly. But it took a little effort to think it.

On Friday, Mr. Mayhew's newspaper interview was the big topic of conversation. "I don't want to talk about it," he warned us that morning. So we didn't mention it to him. But everyone agreed, at home and at school, that the interview was one of the most moving newspaper pieces they had ever read—especially the part where he talked about lying all night beside the Ilu River with a parched throat and a shattered leg, tormented by the sound of the swift-moving stream. I'd noticed that Estelle bought her own copy of the paper in town and carefully cut out the interview to tuck away in her scrapbook.

On my way home from school, I was wondering if it was safe yet to hoist the signal flag on Hawk's Nest. I was starting to miss Sogoji now, and we had a lot to talk about. But maybe not on the hill. Only four days had passed since Frank and I had found the bomb, and army intelligence might still be on the lookout. I could just go over there tomorrow—tell Mom I was going to pay Mrs. Lanski a visit.

Shortly after I turned off the path and started up the road, a black sedan passed me, slowing down for the curve. The emblem on the door was a globe and anchor over the letters *U.S. Marines.* An officer in the passenger seat touched his cap as the car roared past our drive. It had to be going to the Lanskis', the last house on the road.

I stopped abruptly. Why would a military sedan be going there? To ask questions about a suspicious person spotted on the property? My heart started pounding again. Next minute I was running uphill in the same direction the car had taken, with my book satchel bumping against my knees. When the Lanski house came into view, the sedan was parked in front. The driver stood beside it, one foot on the running board, smoking a cigarette. He wore a khaki uniform and an overseas cap. I had just decided to keep out of sight when from the house came an earsplitting scream.

23

WESTERN UNION

The scream buzzed in my fingers and toes. The driver took his foot off the running board and the cigarette out of his mouth, but otherwise he didn't seem surprised. Shortly after, two people came to the door: Mr. Lanski and the officer I'd seen in the front seat of the car. He shook Mr. Lanski's hand and touched the bill of his cap in a salute. Then he turned smartly and marched down the steps.

That's when I understood what must have happened. The book satchel slid out of my hand as the sedan backed around and roared away. Slowly I walked to the porch and climbed the steps. The front door was open a crack, so I pushed it open all the way and walked in.

Mrs. Lanski had collapsed on the floor in the bedroom, her head in her husband's lap. An amazing sight: I'd heard of the mountain coming to Mohammed, but this was like a mountain of curls and ribbons *falling* on the poor old prophet. Mr. Lanski's hand was on her shoulder, stroking awkwardly as she sobbed.

He glanced my way, and even his eyes looked numb. He pointed to the telegram on the floor. "You'd best show that to your sister."

I picked it up. The words were printed on one long strip of paper, cut and pasted in a small rectangle with a Western Union heading: "We regret to inform you that your son, Private First Class John Jedidiah Lanski . . ." I read it a couple of times before looking up. "'Missing in action'? That means he's not . . ."

"All it means," Mr. Lanski said, "is that there's no—there's no body. He might have been captured. Or not."

"Oh, my boy, my boy!" His wife raised her face, and with all the makeup run together it looked at first like her eyes and mouth were melting. "He was only twenty-one—my boy!" Her head flopped down again and the sobs broke out stronger than ever.

"Hush, Mother. Come on now. Shhh."

I felt a horrible stab that went deep and twisted in my gut: guilt. With all the other excitement, I hadn't been watching on the hill—hadn't even thought of Jed for days. I'd abandoned my post, and as soon as that happened—

But that was crazy, right?

I had to try my voice a couple of times before it would work. "Does Sogoji know?"

"He was in the kitchen; I reckon he heard it all." Mr. Lanski's hand kept stroking his wife's shoulder mechanically, as though it didn't know what else to do. He wasn't up to answering any more questions. I put the telegram on the tea table and left the room.

The kitchen was empty and the backyard, too. I took off running, down the path that led to the creek and a little two-room house.

That's where I found him, in the bedroom, standing in front of the table where his family shrine used to be. The table was empty now; in fact, the whole house was clean as a picked bone, stark white and dead. I'd bet money the bird's nest in the oven was gone, too. Sogoji himself looked different, even from the back. I couldn't figure out how at first, but then it hit me: he was absolutely still. I'd never known him to be still. No matter what he was doing, some part of him always tapped or wiggled or waved. But not now.

I tiptoed forward until I stood right next to him, and he never moved. His hands were together as though there was nothing else to hold on to. Just him, with his honey-toned skin and rounded shoulders and slanted eyes. I stole a glance and caught my breath; his face was wet with tears. They had spilled over and made tracks down his face. I had never seen anybody cry while keeping perfectly still: no shudders or sobs, like Mrs. Lanski's.

As we stood there, not moving or speaking, something very strange happened. Without a move or a noise, everything that he was feeling sloshed into me, like river water into an irrigation channel when the sluice gate opens. It wasn't just a trickle, it was a rush. I didn't have to touch him, because we were touching already. My hands came together, my head went down, and I couldn't help but feel I was helping him pray, to a God he didn't even know.

We didn't say anything on our way back to the house, but at the back door I paused. "If I know my mom, she'll be over soon to ask if there's anything she can do. Better keep out of sight." He nodded. "I've been thinking. If we need to get messages to each other, we should be more careful about it. Don't use the flag for a while. I'll put a box under the observation tower, and if we have any messages, we can put them inside. I'll check the box at least every other day, and you can do the same. But be careful—make *sure* there's nobody prowling around. Okay?"

He hiked his shoulder and wiped his face on it. "Okay."

I reached out quickly and squeezed his hand, then let it go. "We'll start watching again, soon as we can. Jed's just missing in action—he'll be all right. You believe me?"

He didn't answer. When we went into the kitchen, he

picked up a spoon but didn't do anything with it—just stared at me, wide-eyed, as I waved before returning to the bedroom.

Not much had changed. Both Lanskis were still on the floor, but the missus had gone from sobbing to snuffling, while her husband leaned against the armchair with his eyes closed. He opened them when I came in, nodding toward the tea table. I picked up the telegram carefully, as though it might crumble, and went out the front door to retrieve my book satchel.

Mom was in the kitchen opening a jar of home-canned green beans. "My word," she remarked, with a sideways glance at me. "Why haven't you changed your clothes? Were you at the Lanskis'?"

"Uh-huh."

"How's Miss Lula getting along lately?"

The front door slammed and Estelle's voice rang out, "It's a red-letter day! Mr. Hendricks let us go early so they could cover furniture before the painters come tomorrow!"

"You can come and peel potatoes for me, then!" Mom called back.

"Oh, *Mother.* Just give me a minute to relax." The phonograph knob clicked as she put on "Boogie Woogie Bugle Boy of Company B."

"That's not music I'd call relaxing," Mom said to me.

"Just a minute." I headed for the living room. Estelle was dancing to the record as she removed her hat and kicked off her shoes one at a time. Pointing her fingers in a dance step called the Shorty George, she turned toward me. "Hey, what are you so gloomy about?"

I just stood there. Estelle stopped and uneasily tossed a lock of hair out of her eyes. "No kidding, what's up?"

Without a word I handed over the telegram and continued on to the bedroom to change out of my school dress. Next minute I heard Estelle's voice quavering, "Mother!" Then the music stopped, and all I heard for the next five minutes were gasps and sobs.

I was buttoning my overalls when Mom appeared at the bedroom door, pulling on her coat. "I'm going down to the Lanskis' to see if there's anything I can do," she said. "I'll try to be back before six, but please watch the beans." She paused, then walked over and gave me a quick hug. This close, I could see her eyes were all red. "I'm sorry, Hazel. Let's be strong and hope for the best."

"Yes, ma'am."

I went back to the living room, half expecting to see Estelle on the floor, melting, like Mrs. Lanski. But she was upright on the sofa with her stationery box in her lap. Her eyes looked like they'd been rubbed with Vaseline, and when she spoke, her voice sounded like it was pulled through a sieve. "I'm writing a note to Artie. To Mr. Mayhew. Would you do me a big favor and take it to him?"

"Now?"

"No, of course not now. Tomorrow when you go to school."

"Tomorrow's Saturday."

Judging by her face, I thought this was the worst news Estelle had received yet. She started crying—or rather, she started crying again, as weak and pathetic as a hurt kitten. "But he has to know . . . and I just can't face him now; I can't—"

"Okay," I said quickly. "Maybe I can take it to the Hedgecocks' tomorrow if it's not raining or anything."

"Thanks, Hazel. I won't forget it. I feel so—so—" Fresh sobs welled up and Estelle covered her face with her hands. "So mixed *up*." I wondered if I should give her a hug and tell her to be strong. But there was only enough energy in me to go to the kitchen and stir the beans.

Mom didn't even try to keep our spirits up that night.

The next morning, Frank called. None of us were expecting it, since he had only got to Bonneville the day before. While I spooned applesauce on my pancakes and topped it off with a tiny dab of brown sugar, Mom's voice on the phone went from surprise ("Why, Frank!") to suspicion ("Why aren't you at work?") to sadness ("We got some bad news yesterday . . ."). After a moment she said, "Yes, she's in the kitchen having breakfast—what's that? . . . All right, just a minute. Hazel—" I glanced up to see her beckoning to me through the kitchen door.

Slowly I put down my fork and walked to the phone as Mom finished up her part of the conversation. "All right, Frankie, work hard and stay warm. . . . Here she is." She handed over the receiver with a puzzled look and returned to the kitchen.

"Hello?" I said.

"Hi, Hazel, how are you?"

Right away, I knew something was up. He almost never called me by my real name or used that jolly tone of voice when talking to me. "Say," he went on, "I had to tell you. Remember that bobcat you saw on Hawk's Nest, a couple of nights before Christmas?"

We both knew Annie Billings might be listening on the party line, so I didn't blurt out, "What bobcat?" Instead I said carefully, "Uh-huh."

"Well, I had to tell you. I was talking to one of the guys last night and he saw one, too. It was on January third. How about that?"

"Oh," I said. How about that?

"Yeah, he says other people have seen them, all over northern California and Oregon. So keep your eyes peeled. You'd better believe *I* will. I don't have to tell you to be careful—you know they're dangerous."

"Okay. I'll be careful."

Frank dropped the fake heartiness. "Tough news about Jed."

"Uh-huh."

"Well, that's all I wanted to tell you. Keep your nose clean."

He signed off with, "So long, Nut." I hung up the phone,

wondering if Mrs. Billings would spend the rest of the weekend worried sick about bobcats. That wasn't my problem, though; my problem was that the to-do over our bomb discovery wasn't local. People had been seeing explosions in the sky all over the Northwest. That meant the enemy had some kind of program under way, and *that* meant the government might still be interested in our neighborhood. I'd better get another warning to Sogoji: it wasn't over yet.

But when I started for the bedroom to get dressed, the door opened and Estelle came out, wrapped in her bathrobe. Mom had let her sleep in that morning, but it didn't help—her eyes were puffier than the day before, as though she'd cried even in her sleep. "It's not raining," she told me.

At first I couldn't think what the weather had to do with anything but then remembered her note to Mr. Mayhew. Great—a Dear John letter *and* a warning to be delivered as soon as possible, and they didn't even lie in the same direction. And though it wasn't raining now, a gloomy layer of clouds and a damp feel hung over the morning.

Still, I had sort of promised. "Okay." I sighed. "Give me a minute."

24

IN THE RAIN

The clouds were just beginning to leak a cold, steady drizzle. Mom objected to me running errands in the cold and wet until Estelle talked her into it. Then she insisted that I take a handkerchief and not stay out more than an hour—as if I'd want to! Half an hour later I left the house with Estelle's letter in one pocket and a warning note for Sogoji in the other, tucked inside an oilcloth zipper pouch I had found in Frank's camping equipment.

As I climbed up to Hawk's Nest, a company of marines fell in behind me. They were looking for Jed—no, they already knew from my scouting work that he was in a POW camp, and we were on our way to rescue him. Nobody knew the island like I did. My nerves of steel and sure sense of direction gave them confidence, though the company captain insisted that I get out of the way when the shooting started. "We can't afford to lose you, Hazelee...."

At the corner of the observation tower, I stuck a hand in my pocket and grabbed the silver dollar, squeezing so hard the rim cut into my palm. The marines behind me melted away.

None of it helped—not the tower, not the imagining, not all the doing-my-part in the world had kept Jed safe. I hiked myself up on the lower platform and slumped there like a sack of potatoes, one hand still clutching the silver dollar. Tears welled up inside me, like somebody had turned the faucet on. I took a big gasping breath and out they came, in waves and sobs. Before long the handkerchief Mom made me bring was sopping.

When it was over, I felt lighter—but anything feels lighter when it's empty.

I wasn't much good to anybody just sitting there in the rain. While poking around for a place to hide the oilcloth pouch, I discovered that Sogoji had already been here: wedged between the boards under the second-tier platform was a note wrapped in wax paper to keep out some of the wet. I unwrapped it and found HAZL written on the outside. Inside was a drawing of a mountain with Japanese characters. It looked familiar—then

I remembered seeing the same design on the card in his family shrine. The wedding card, he called it. Below, he'd written a translation, but it took me a while to figure it out: THE FLOERS FAD. THE MOUNTN IS FOREVR. The flowers fade. The mountain is forever.

That's nice, I thought. He probably meant it for comfort, but who cared how long the mountain lasted if the people you loved weren't around to enjoy it? I folded up the paper and stuffed it in my pocket, along with the handkerchief.

Then I hung the pouch from a nail sticking out under the platform. It wasn't exactly hidden, but it wasn't obvious either. I set off downhill, mission halfway accomplished.

From the Lanskis' it was a mile and a half to the Hedgecocks'. There were a lot of shortcuts I could have taken, maybe looking for scrap metal on the way. But the thought of hunting things in the woods made me a little queasy, now that I knew the kind of things out there to be found. So I kept to the path leading back to Anderson Brothers Orchard, then followed the road all the way to Ash Grove.

The Hedgecocks lived at the edge of town, in the last house on Cascade Avenue. Mrs. Hedgecock was collecting her mail from the box when I trotted up. "Good heavens, child, why are you traipsing around on a day like this? You'll catch your death."

"It's not so cold." I'd been running to keep warm. "How are you, Mrs. Hedgecock? Have you heard from Mike?"

The lady sifted through her mail and shook her head. "Not

lately. He's in France, that's all we know. Everybody thinks the Germans are about to surrender. I pray to God they will—Hitler's got to know he's beat."

"Uh-huh." My eyes strayed to the banner in their window. There were two stars on it—a blue one for Mike and a gold one for Bobby, who was killed in Italy. I thought of a gold star going up in the Lanskis' window, and a chill ran across my shoulders. "I have a note for Mr. Mayhew. Is he home?"

An odd look crossed Mrs. Hedgecock's face—if I didn't know better, I might have called it a disgusted look. "He's home. In fact, he's probably still in bed."

"He does sleep a lot," I said politely.

"Do tell. You may as well get him up and let him know his breakfast is on the stove."

I followed a rock path around to the garage, where Mr. Mayhew lived in the upstairs apartment originally built for Mrs. Hedgecock's departed mother. I climbed the stairs and knocked on the door—then knocked a little louder to be heard over the radio. The cold crept up on me and I sneezed again, pulling the handkerchief out of my pocket just in time.

Mr. Mayhew was up and dressed, but not fully awake yet. "Hazel." He yawned. "What's going on?"

"My sister asked me to give you this letter." Stuffing the handkerchief back in one pocket, I pulled Estelle's note from the other, holding it so he could see his name on the envelope.

His voice lightened up. "She did? Hand it over." He opened

the screen, and I noticed he hadn't shaved yet. Through the doorway I could see a kitchen table cluttered with newspapers and coffee cups and cigarette butts. "Thanks."

"Mrs. Hedgecock says your breakfast is on the stove."

"Okay." After a pause he added, "I'll see you Monday, kid." I took the hint, clattered down the steps, and started the long walk home.

It wasn't until that night, while getting ready for bed, that I remembered Sogoji's note. But it wasn't in my overalls. After searching all the pockets twice, I remembered putting it in the same pocket as the handkerchief and blowing my nose at Mr. Mayhew's door. With a slam, the truth hit me: the note must have fallen out when I pulled out the handkerchief. When I left, it was probably lying right there on the stair landing in plain sight. What if Mr. Mayhew picked it up, and noticed the Japanese characters, and decided to call army intelligence? For a minute I wanted to run like mad to the Hedgecocks' and search for the note. But it was probably too late.

How could I do something that *stupid*?

Sunday was miserable, for a lot of reasons. We all stayed home from church: I was sneezing and coughing, Estelle was still crying, and Mom just ran out of steam. As though to make up for it, she kept the vaporizer on all day, filling the house with the nose-biting smell of Vicks as we slept off and on like soldiers with battle fatigue.

When I was awake, I worried, even though maybe there was

nothing to worry about. Mr. Mayhew could have walked past that note without seeing it. Or maybe it blew off the porch and the ink washed out, leaving only a piece of trash for Mrs. Hedgecock to throw away. The thing to do was rest up so I could go to school on Monday and get the score, as Frank would say.

That night Mom took my temperature twice without finding any fever, and I fell asleep with a nose that felt almost clear by the power of Vicks.

Monday dawned sunny and a little warmer. Estelle decided to go to work and I insisted on going to school, to Mom's surprise. "Since you don't show any fever, I guess you can. But my word—I never thought you'd fight me *not* to stay home."

On the walk to school, I worked out a plan based on three possible situations. One: If Mr. Mayhew showed me the paper and demanded an explanation, I would say it was a joke between Frank and me, based on a code we had worked out. I'd forgotten it was in my pocket—ha, ha. Two: If he didn't say anything but looked at me suspiciously through the day, I would try very hard to look like I was not trying at all to act perfectly normal. Three: If he had already called the FBI and they were waiting for me outside the schoolhouse, I would square my shoulders and stand my ground and give them the secret code story.

The only possibility I wasn't prepared for was if nothing happened. But that's what happened: nothing.

Mr. Mayhew did seem a little anxious. He handed out arithmetic tests and sentences to diagram in the morning:

"midyear exams," he called them, though he hadn't bothered to warn us the week before. While we worked, he read newspapers, tapping his pencil on the desk. That got on my nerves, as edgy as I was already. He gave us longer recesses and raced through the afternoon reading of *Tom Sawyer* as though in a hurry to get it over with. And he let us out early. When Sherman protested, Mr. Mayhew said, "It's sunny outside. You kids need some fresh air after being cooped up over the holidays."

On his way out the door, Sherman grumbled that it was probably the teacher who needed fresh air after the holidays. "No kidding," Owen broke in. "After the way he's been carrying on with Hazel's sister."

The next minute, my book satchel had met his stomach hard enough to knock him down. Not enough to keep him down, though: he was on his feet in no time but couldn't bring himself to beat up on a girl. By the time the yelling was over, I discovered I'd come out ahead. "Glad you clobbered him," Sherman told me before setting off for home.

Ivy strolled up and put her arm through mine. "I haven't heard anything bad about Estelle," she cooed. "Everybody thinks she was just being nice to a soldier, and I'm sure she feels terrible about Jed."

"Sure," Margie chimed in. "I would, too—just *terrible*."

"Want to come over and listen to records?" Ivy offered.

I turned down the invitation—something told me they only wanted to know exactly how terrible Estelle felt. But on the way home I wondered, for the first time, what it might be like to spend an afternoon with a bunch of other girls, reading movie magazines and trying out new dance steps. And experimenting with hairstyles and gabbing about boys—I'd give them an earful about Frank and his pals.

Soon after I turned onto our road, a big green sedan rolled up beside me. The driver leaned over and rolled down the window. "Afternoon, miss."

I noticed he didn't say *little girl*. "Hello."

"Going home from school?"

I nodded.

"Is Mr. Arthur Mayhew your teacher?"

After a pause, I nodded again, fear grabbing hold of my stomach. The man looked to be middle-aged, dressed in a slick-looking gray suit with an old fedora on his head—a plainclothes agent?

"I've been looking all over for the schoolhouse," he said. "Can you tell me where it is?"

Mr. Mayhew must have called somebody! Like an FBI agent, who'd come to collect a note with Japanese writing on it! "The school?" I croaked, my mouth as dry as dust.

"Yeah, the school. Where you said you just came from."

Why do you want to know? That's what I longed to ask, but it probably wouldn't be smart. "You . . . you can't get there from here."

"How's that?" The friendly mask he wore began to slip.

"I mean, not in a car. There's a path back that way—" I waved in a direction that wasn't anywhere in particular. "I've got to get home. My mother's expecting me."

"Hey, wait—" I was already marching up the road, and he decided not to press it. In a minute I heard the gears grind as he shifted into reverse and swung the auto around with a jerk. It sounded like the car itself was exasperated with me.

Not that I could spare any sympathy for the car's feelings or the driver's. My thoughts were in an uproar, wondering what he might be after. And did I throw off any suspicion? In a pig's eye: I'd more likely stirred it up.

25

THE GAME'S UP

What I'd told the stranger in the green sedan was half right: my mother was home, but she wasn't expecting me this early. "Not *again*."

"The teacher isn't feeling too good." I wandered to the refrigerator to pour a glass of milk but didn't drink it. Instead I drifted over to the sink and rinsed off some dirty dishes, wondering what excuse I could make to get over to the Lanskis' house.

"Hmmm." Mom had just set the top crust of an apple pie and was trimming the edges with quick jabs of a paring knife. "Mrs.

Clark told me today that he asked for an advance on his paycheck. I wish he'd tried harder to get his pension. I was about to write to the army myself, but I guess there's no point now." She put down the knife and began crimping the edge of the piecrust with her fingers. "You seem awfully fidgety this afternoon."

I plopped down at the table. "No, I'm not. Have you found another teacher yet?"

"No luck so far. I may have to talk to Mrs. Weatherby."

"Not Mrs. Weatherby!" This was an old lady who had taught everybody in the valley at one time or another and substituted even now in a pinch. She was at least eighty—she wore black stockings rolled over her knees and smelled like stale saltines. The way she taught was by lining up four or five kids in front of the class and drilling them on times tables or spelling words. If you missed, you had to turn around and face the blackboard.

"Well, I'm at my wit's end," Mom said. "If all else fails, we could pile everybody in a pickup truck and run you down to Hood River School every day."

"That wouldn't be so bad." I was thinking of Margie Holmes bouncing along in a truck bed with the rain wilting her latest hairdo.

"When you change your clothes, I have an errand for you."

"Aw, Mom—"

"Don't sass me, young lady. I have a couple of pies in the oven that are just about done. I want you to take one to the Lanskis'."

"Oh. Okay." I tried not to sound too eager, but this was perfect. Mom to the rescue!

When the pies were done, she insisted on letting them settle, but finally I was on the way carrying a box with a pie nestled inside. My load made it impossible to climb the hill, so I took the long way up the road.

Mr. Lanski's pickup was gone and no one answered my knock, even though I could hear voices. After setting the box on the porch I opened the front door a crack, meaning to holler, "Anybody home?" The radio was turned way down and Mrs. Lanski seemed to be talking on the telephone. Not talking, that is, but wailing. "Oh, Bernice, you just don't know. . . . Yes, every day gets worse. I can't stop crying." Her voice rose and quivered. "I'll tell you, Bernice, I've never had a mean thought for anybody, but right now I'd like to see Japan wiped off the face of the map. . . ."

I slipped in and tiptoed past the bedroom on the way to the kitchen, but she didn't appear to notice me. The kitchen table was loaded with food: two cakes, a ham, a pot roast, and three scalloped potato casseroles. Of course it was nice of the neighbors to show their support, but the thought of people coming around made me nervous. From the talk I'd been hearing, it was way too early for Sogoji to be accidentally discovered.

I began to hear a noise from the backyard: a steady chop! chop! chop! Through the window I saw Sogoji splitting logs in quick, jerky movements, like a mechanical man.

He stacked up an armload of wood, but instead of taking it into the house, he set off in the opposite direction.

I ran to the back door and pulled it open. "Hey!"

Startled, he whirled around. His smile popped out like the sun from clouds. "Hazel!"

"Where are you going?"

"To Father's house. Why do you come?"

"My mother sent a pie over. Why are you going down there?"

He just sighed and jerked his head in the direction of the woods, meaning I should join him.

Silently we trotted down to the clearing, where he went straight into the house and dropped his load of wood by the stove. Quickly I took in the canned goods stacked on the table, a pallet on the floor, and a pot on one of the burners.

"What gives? Are you living here now?"

He blew on the fire to make it blaze up, then added a few sticks of wood and closed the firebox door. "It's best."

"Best for who?"

He didn't want to say. "Lula-san . . . she has trouble."

"I get it. Would it help if you set fire to her back?"

Sogoji didn't smile. In fact, he looked even more unhappy, as he lifted the lid on the iron pot. The smell of pork and beans filled the room.

"Who needs her, anyway?" I said. "After the war, you should move to town and open a restaurant: Sogoji's all-American cooking."

He just looked at me, puzzled. "A joke?"

"Yeah. But not very funny, I guess."

He replaced the lid and sat down—or dropped down—on the pallet. After a minute I went over to sit beside him. "She'll get over it. She always does, right?"

"Right." He nodded but didn't seem too convinced.

"You want to hear a story?" I asked, hoping to make him feel better. He shrugged, but I took it for a yes.

"This is kind of a fairy tale, only there's no magic in it. Once upon a time, a mama duck hatched a nest of ducklings, but one of them was so ugly all the others pecked his feathers off until he was even uglier. They ran him out of the nest and he went from one place to another, trying to find a home. But the other animals just laughed at him. When winter came, he curled up in a hollow tree and hoped to die.

"But he didn't die. When the weather changed and his tree budded, he crept out and found himself next to a pond. The first thing he saw were swans paddling around in the water, and they were so beautiful—" Here I felt my eyes sting and a funny pinching sensation in my nose. "They were so beautiful all he could do was stare at them. And then he called out, 'Oh, beautiful birds, I know I'm too ugly to swim with you, but could I just stay a little longer and look?' And one of them answered back: 'Of course you can stay. You're one of us.' And when he stretched out his long neck and looked into the pond, he saw his reflection. And that was the first he knew he was a swan himself."

Abruptly I drew my knees up and put my head down. Nice going: I'd meant to help him feel better but only made myself feel worse. After a minute I felt a touch on my back like the brush of a wing tip. "That's a good story, Hazel."

Wrong story, Hazel, I told myself. He'd been chased out of one pond, but there wasn't any other for him.

"Well, anyway." I raised my head with a final sniff. "That's not what I came over for. We have to make some plans." I told him of the green sedan and the nosy questions asked by the man in it but managed not to say how I might have left his note on Mr. Mayhew's doorstep. "I don't know what it's all about, but as long as strangers are poking around the neighborhood, we've got to be extra careful. You need a real hideout."

"Hazel." He sighed. "If they find, they find. It is *shikato-ganai*."

"What's that?"

"Something that must happen. Can't be helped."

I felt like shaking him—this was no time to go Japanese. "We've got serious work to do! We could be using our tower to watch for those bombs if they'd just leave us alone. But we don't have to take this lying down—we've got to have a plan."

"'We'?" He half smiled at me.

"Think about it: suppose you've just cooked your dinner and you're sitting here with a bowl in your hands. Suddenly you hear shouting outside!" His eyes widened in alarm. "You look through the crack in the window boards and see flashlight beams—at least two! So you know it's not Mr. Lanski. What do you do? Where can you hide?"

He looked around the room frantically. "Under the bed!" When I stared at him, dumbstruck, he laughed: chk-chk-chk.

"No joke," I said sternly. "This could really happen."

He sighed again. "Okay, Hazel."

"If the G-men do come down here, it'll be hard to explain why the stove is fired up. Maybe we could slice up some apples and spread them on a tray so it'll look like the stove's being used to dry them. Anything you're not using you'll have to keep hidden. Find a place to stash dishes and stuff. If you have to make a quick escape, you can go out the back door. Let's see if we can get it unboarded."

He hauled himself up from the pallet. I was afraid we would need a hammer to claw the nails out of the door, but the boards had rotted enough to give way with a little wiggling. Sogoji followed me into the backyard, now a tangle of vines and brush. "So you're out of the house. Where do you hide?"

"Cellar?" He pointed to a wooden door half hidden under the rampaging ivy vines. I hadn't even known it was there.

"First place they'd look. I don't suppose you have any secret tunnels in it?" He shook his head. "No time to dig one. Do you have any caves or hollow trees around here?"

"I don't think . . ."

"Just a minute." I took off toward the creek; the sound of running water had given me an idea. At the bank I searched downstream until I found the deep pool by the stand of bamboo.

"This'll do in a pinch. If somebody's looking for you, head straight for this spot and jump in."

"But—"

"Before you do, grab a piece of bamboo so you can lie on your back and keep your head underwater and still breathe. See?" I broke off a length of dry bamboo stalk and tilted my head back with the tube in my mouth. "Terry Lee could stay underwater for hours."

"But it's *cold.* . . ."

"I know, but you could last for five minutes. That might be enough. Anyway, it's just until we can think of something better."

The sun had already slipped behind the treetops, and the winter dusk was galloping on. "I'd better go—meet me on the hill at three o'clock tomorrow and we'll work on our plans. But be careful, just in case somebody's watching for you."

He walked me to the path, where I squeezed his hand before taking off. "See ya!"

"See ya," he repeated. I turned where the path made a bend and saw him there, still waving.

Before I left the house next morning, Mom called, "Hold on a minute. Take this to Mr. Mayhew, please." She wiped her hands on a dish towel and picked up an envelope from her desk. "It's his paycheck, so be very careful not to lose it. And tell him the school board would like to talk to him this week. Mrs. Clark will call him."

I walked through the woods with a sense of dread, my shoulders up and my neck pinched as though two fingers were back there, squeezing hard. At school, everybody was on time except Sherman—strange, because Sherman was working on a perfect attendance record. I handed over the envelope with the check first thing, meanwhile watching Mr. Mayhew suspiciously to see if he was watching *me* suspiciously. But all he did was open the envelope for a quick look. Then he smiled and told me to take my seat.

I didn't smile back. It was hard to see him as anything but trouble now, in spite of his war record. Besides, he'd survived Guadalcanal to take Estelle out to dances, while Jed was missing in action. Of course that wasn't his fault, but there it was.

Everyone stood for the pledge, and in the middle of "the republic for which it stands," the sound of an approaching car made me look out the window. "One nation" stuck in my throat: pulling up in front of the schoolhouse was a green sedan, and on the dashboard was a beat-up fedora.

I glanced at Mr. Mayhew, who was staring out the window instead of at the flag, his hand over his heart. By the time the pledge petered out, with only a few voices remaining on "liberty and justice for all," I knew he wasn't expecting this any more than I was.

Another car pulled up in a spray of gravel: a black sedan with HOOD RIVER COUNTY SHERIFF on the door and a bunch of people inside. "That's Sherman in the back!" Owen burst out. "And his brother!"

Without asking permission, Owen bolted for the schoolhouse door with Marvin right behind. The other boys followed. I saw Margie glance at Mr. Mayhew before leading a stampede of girls. The whole student body was in the yard when Sherman popped out of the sheriff's car, yelling, "You'll never guess! The game's up! Mr. Mayhew is a—"

"Put a lid on it, son." A man in a black suit, emerging from the passenger side of the car, caught Sherman by the collar. "Okay, kids, we need to talk to your teacher. I'm Lieutenant Throckmorton, FBI."

But Mr. Mayhew wasn't in the yard. When Gladys and I ran back inside the schoolroom, it was empty. Mr. Mayhew is a—what was he? My heart was swollen to the size of a watermelon.

"Look!" Owen shouted, and everybody ran outside again.

Owen was pointing at two figures coming out of the woods: the driver of the green sedan and Mr. Mayhew. Not until they reached the school yard did we see the handcuffs on the teacher's wrists.

Roger was the first to find his voice. "Holy cow. This is the best school year we *ever* had!"

26

WHEN THE WORST HAPPENS

The school board—or the part represented by my mother, Mrs. Clark, and Mrs. Holmes—didn't share Roger's opinion. During the half hour it took to round up those three, Mr. Mayhew was removed by a deputy and the investigator (who tipped his fedora to me on his way out). That was good for Mr. Mayhew, or else the ladies of the school board might have busted his other leg once they'd heard the whole story from Lieutenant Throckmorton of the FBI.

It turned out that the man they had honored as a war hero, and supplied with room and board and allowed to teach their children, had only stayed in the army long enough for basic training. He deserted as soon as his outfit shipped out for Guadalcanal. Arthur Mayhew wasn't even his real name—he'd taken it from an acquaintance who was later killed in action.

For two years he had been on the lam, taking different jobs under different names and cutting out before anyone became suspicious. Only he got a little careless this time and gave that fatal interview to the Hood River paper.

"I offered him fifteen bucks for it," Sherman's brother said.

That's what brought Mr. Mayhew down—I had to wonder if he needed money for gifts like nylon stockings. The lieutenant figured he meant to skip out as soon as he got his advance check from the school board (the members of the school board, once they heard that, looked mad enough to chew up the desks they were sitting at). Unfortunately for Mr. Mayhew, a soldier who had really served in Guadalcanal happened to be visiting his aunt in Hood River when the interview appeared. It sounded fishy to him, especially the part about lying all night beside the swift waters of the Ilu River. The veteran had spent enough time beside the Ilu to know that it was little more than a mud stream. There were other mistakes, too, like describing the signal flares used on the island as blue when they were really green.

The veteran called army intelligence, and they notified the FBI to put one of their plainclothes men on it. Once the investigator discovered that "Arthur Mayhew" was not who he claimed to be, the wheels of justice started turning.

Owen asked about Mr. Mayhew's bum leg. "Anybody ever seen it?" Lieutenant Throckmorton asked. "Anybody notice a crooked bone or a scar? He might have banged it up himself—a lot of deserters do that—or he might have faked the whole thing. It's not that hard to fake a limp. Any more questions?"

Nobody raised a hand. The school board was so humiliated I think they just wanted to get the ordeal over as soon as possible. Lieutenant Throckmorton picked up his hat from the desk. "It's not an uncommon story, sad to say. Not that you should suspect every veteran you don't know of being a con man. Just be aware and inform your local police of any suspicious behavior."

By the time he left, it was past eleven o'clock. I had to stick around for another half hour while the school board discussed how outraged they were and made plans for an emergency meeting of all the parents. Since we sure wouldn't be having school the next day, the kids were a lot happier than the grown-ups.

Especially me. My heart, now shrunk back to its normal size, was singing as I rode home in the backseat of Mrs. Clark's car. My fears had melted away like frost—there was nobody investigating me, or Sogoji, or the Lanskis. The Japs had exploded no more balloon bombs overhead and I had a feeling Jed was alive. Everything was going to be okay.

After lunch and an hour's worth of phone calls, Mom said, "I have a splitting headache. I'm going to lie down for an hour, and if I'm not up by four, please light the burner under that pot of soup on the stove."

"Yes, ma'am." I tried to look sorry, but her splitting headache would make it a lot easier to meet Sogoji on the hill at three, like we'd planned. The rain had started again and the temperature had dropped to around freezing; if she knew I was going out, Mom would have said, "After you just got over a cold? I should think *not.*" But she didn't notice anything from the bedroom with an ice pack on her head.

Wrapped in two sweaters and Frank's old yellow rain slicker, I climbed the hill backed up by a squad of jungle commandos, on their way at last to meet the mysterious ally who had been their silent ears for so long. This is Sogoji, men—a true-blue American, not like certain deserters I could name—and I expect every one of you to treat him with the respect his deeds deserve. Our next mission is to rescue Private Jed Lanski of the U.S. Marines. . . .

Humming "The Marines' Hymn," I crested the hill—

Where the person waiting under the tower was not Sogoji.

"Afternoon, Hazel," Mr. Lanski said. He was sitting on the lowest tier, holding an umbrella. Speechless, I stared at him.

"Some structure you two built up here. Must be a fine view from the top. Of course, it's exactly the kind of thing I warned you about."

Something was very, very wrong. My voice cracked with fear. "Where's Sogoji?"

"Well. Why don't you get out of the rain first?"

He shifted a little and I climbed up beside him. "Where's Sogoji?"

"He's in the county jail, down at Hood River. I hate to be the one to tell—"

The worst happens when you don't expect it, Daddy had said.

"No, he's not!" I yelled. "Mr. Mayhew's the one in jail!"

"I don't know about that, but—what are you—hey, stop it!"

I was beating the boards with my fists, then I was pulling at my braids, all the time spouting stormy tears. When his words didn't stop me, he dropped the umbrella, grabbed my shoulders, and gave a little shake. "What's got into you?"

"I didn't mean to do it! I didn't mean to!"

"Mean to do what? Come on, talk sense."

Between sobs, I told him about carrying Sogoji's note over to the Hedgecocks' and accidentally dropping it where it could be found. Near the end of the confession, Mr. Lanski started shaking his head. "All right, settle down. *Settle down,* I said. You didn't have anything to do with it."

"Huh?" Startled, I forgot my manners.

"It was my wife. Mrs. Lanski tipped off the police."

For a minute I was struck dumb again.

He leaned over to pick up his umbrella and shake it out. "Ever since we got the news about Jed, see, she can't stand the sight of Sogoji. She made his life miserable when I wasn't around, so he stayed out of her way as much as possible. I expected it to blow over—"

"But it's not Sogoji's fault that Jed's missing in action!"

"Sure, I know that. She knows it, too, but some folks just let bitterness eat into 'em until it destroys their common sense. Common kindness, too, sometimes."

"She'll be *sorry*." And how I wanted her to be sorry—at that moment, I wanted her back to ache and her stomach to shrink and those bouncy yellow curls to fall limp—maybe even fall out.

"She's sorry already, I think. After the police left, she got kind of hysterical and I had to slip a little something in her Ovaltine to put her out."

"But why the police? Sogoji didn't do anything, and besides, it's okay to be Japanese in America now, isn't it? I mean, legally?"

"That's just it. We're not sure how legal Sogoji is, since he didn't stand up and be counted with his own people. The way the deputy explained it to me, he's a ward of the state until that's settled."

"When did they come and get him?" I asked in a very small voice.

"About ten this morning. He was down at his house, but he must have heard us coming because the place was empty when we got there." Mr. Lanski shook his head. "It didn't take long to find him, and a good thing, too, because he was so scared he jumped into the creek and held himself underwater with a bamboo stalk in his mouth. Loony thing to do—don't know where he got that idea. . . ."

I couldn't hide my expression, and he couldn't help seeing it. "Wait a minute," he said. "From you?"

Miserably, I nodded. "People do it in the comics all the time."

After a pause, he sighed. "This is real life, sister. If he'd stayed in the water much longer, we might never have thawed him out."

"Will he be all right?"

"He will if he takes care of himself."

"But he *can't* take care of himself!" I burst out. "He's so shy, and he can't read very well, and he doesn't know anybody, and—"

He held up his hand and studied me for such a long time it made me squirm. "Maybe he can manage better than we think. Looks like we'll have to give him that chance."

My tears started up again—slow tears this time. Mr. Lanski pulled a handkerchief out of his hip pocket and awkwardly passed it over. "Wh-wh-what's going to happen to him?" I asked.

"They're sending him to some kind of detention center in San Francisco tomorrow. After that—"

"Tomorrow!"

"Yep. I'm going to pack some things to take to him in the morning. The train leaves at eight forty-five."

I started getting an idea then—a wild idea at first thought, and second and third thoughts, too, but it was worth a try. "Can I go down there with you? To say goodbye to him?"

Mr. Lanski cleared his throat. "Yeah, I figured you'd want to. But don't jump the gun. Feelings being what they are against the Japanese, I expect I'll be in bad odor around here for a while. You might, too. If you'd rather lay low, it stops right here. I could give Sogoji a message from you. Think about it."

I blew my nose on his handkerchief, louder than intended: honk! "When should I come over tomorrow morning?"

"No need. I'll stop by for you."

"I'd rather come over. When?"

He shrugged. "Have it your way. Seven-thirty."

I hopped down to the ground, slipping a little on the mud. "I'll have to think of something to tell my mother."

Rain veiled his face as he raised the umbrella over his head. For a minute, he looked just like Jed. "If I were you, I'd tell her the truth."

That's exactly what I did, after Mom returned from the parents' meeting that night. First I let her take her shoes off and stretch out on the sofa, sighing, "I can't take one more crisis."

I hoped that wasn't true, because of one more crisis to come.

One good thing about the uproar over Mr. Mayhew: Mom

had used up all her feelings on it. She seemed as dry as a well in August when I told my story. When it was over, Mom stared at the ceiling while the seconds went by, one by one.

"How long have you known . . . this person?" she asked then.

"Sogoji? Since October."

More seconds passed. "And what is it you want to do?"

"Go to Hood River with Mr. Lanski and say goodbye to him."

Tick-tock, tick-tock. Abruptly Mom pulled herself upright and shook her head. "I'm partly to blame. I've been so busy with Citizens' League and ration coupons and the school board I haven't had time to look out for my own children. Tomorrow I'm resigning from the school board." While I was trying to fig-ure out if this was permission or not, Mom stood up, wrapped an arm around my neck, and crushed me to her bosom. "You're getting so tall, Hazel." I knew what she meant—I came almost up to her chin now. She rocked me back and forth for a minute, and I had to admit it felt good. "What am I going to do with you?"

Later that night, Estelle came over to sit cross-legged on the floor beside my pillow. She must have heard me sniffling. "At least you probably pick your friends better than I do," she said.

I dried my eyes on a corner of the bedsheet. "Mr. Mayhew had us all fooled."

"Sometimes people want to be fooled. And the war doesn't leave a lot of room for mistakes. It tells us how to think and feel . . . and I guess we have to think and feel that way to get the job done. But if anyone has a chance to do some simple kindness—like you did, making friends with this poor boy—I think they should do it."

"Thanks." I sniffed. I didn't feel that kind, especially if Sogoji ended up with pneumonia. But I was going to try to make it up to him anyway.

27

THE MOUNTAIN IS FOREVER

Mom and Estelle were still in bed when I left the house early the next morning, lugging my knapsack and a little cardboard suitcase I used to take on visits to Grandma Anderson. Loaded with half a dozen of my favorite books, plus a thick folder of "Terry and the Pirates" episodes cut out of the Sunday paper, the suitcase slowed me down a little. But still I arrived in plenty of time to stow it under a tarp in the truck bed before Mr. Lanski could see it and ask questions.

Then I waited on the front porch, shivering. The house was very quiet; not even the faintest sound of a radio came through the windows. I was beginning to wonder if Lula-san still had to take "a little something" in her Ovaltine when the door opened and Mr. Lanski stepped out on the porch. "Glad you're on time," he said.

He had brought along some biscuits wrapped in a newspaper and offered me one after we climbed into the truck. "The missus made 'em last night," he remarked while backing out of the driveway. "Not bad, for a woman who hasn't cooked in eight years."

"Are you going to get another maid?"

He merely snorted in reply and said nothing more as the truck followed the highway curves and grades down to Hood River. I took another biscuit, glancing at the newsprint wrapper. It looked like the letters page. *No More Enemy Aliens in Our Valley,* ran one headline, and another: *Once a Jap, Always a Jap.* But then I saw this one: *All Men Made in God's Image.* Skipping to the end of the letter, I read, *Many have fought and bled in the American armed forces. If they are willing to die for their country, should they not be allowed to live here?* I tore off that corner of the newspaper and stuck it in my pocket, then stared out the window at frosty fields and rounded hills and cozy houses with smoke puffing from the chimneys. I'd never known any home but this valley, but at that moment it didn't feel like home at all.

Hood River seemed to be just waking up when we arrived. "Everybody's slow to move, these damp cold days," Mr. Lanski remarked while pulling into the gravel lot beside the county jail. A deputy was coming out of the diner across the street, picking his teeth; he nodded to Mr. Lanski as he approached.

"That teacher fella's gone already," I heard him say as I slid off the front seat and onto the gravel. "The army done packed him off to Fort Lewis, the low-down coward. . . ." Wrapping the last two biscuits in what was left of the torn newspaper, I crept around to the back of the truck bed, stepped up on the running board, and pulled my suitcase from under the tarp. While finding a place inside it to stash the biscuit, I noticed that the deputy didn't seem to be mad at Mr. Lanski—no words like "Jap lover" spiked the conversation. The big news was Mr. Mayhew; maybe everybody had used up their outrage on him, like my mom had.

"Okay," Mr. Lanski called to me as the deputy walked on toward the jail, a ring of keys jangling in his hand. "He says we can go in. Sogoji's up and dressed, and they'll let us have at least thirty minutes before—what's that?"

I'd closed the suitcase and jumped down, too quick. He came around the back end of the trunk and caught sight of one cardboard corner poking out from under the tarp.

I pulled out the suitcase, squared my shoulders, and looked him right in the eye. "I'm going with him. At least as far as San Francisco. I've got enough money saved for a ticket."

He slapped the side panel of the pickup bed with an exasperated grunt. "And what would your mother think of that?"

"She wouldn't care. Last night she asked me, 'What am I going to do with you?'"

"I think that's what people call a rhetorical question. Or did you two talk this over?" I didn't answer. "Come on—you're twelve years old, right? Old enough to know a crazy scheme when you see it?"

Never taking my eyes from his, I said, "Sogoji needs me. I'm his only friend."

"He'll be with his own people, and that's—"

"*I'm* his people!" I cried.

We stared at each other for half a minute, me trying hard not to blink. Finally he said, "Okay. You talk to him. Don't mention what you've got in mind—just try to get a handle on how he feels. I'll go first—"

"Let me go first."

Mr. Lanski rolled his eyes and slapped the panel again. Just as I suspected—he'd probably intended to tell Sogoji what to say before I could get to him. "Okay, but listen to me. You *can't* go with him. Even if your mother allowed it, which she won't, the U.S. government, the army, and the state of Oregon wouldn't let you. See? They're all bigger than you. This world is bigger than you. You may think you can change the things you don't like about it, but believe me, sister, you can't."

I opened my mouth to protest, but he went on:

"However. If you let Sogoji think there's a chance, and he gets it in his head that you're going along, and his heart breaks one more time when they put him on that train by himself, I'll turn you over my knee and tan your hide, even though you're not my kid. Understand?"

I couldn't meet his eyes anymore. The suitcase slid out of my hand and flopped to one side with the weight of books and comics. I felt my lip trembling, and bit down on it so hard a little blood welled up. Silently I turned and walked toward the jail.

The deputy must have been expecting me, because he let me into the cell block without any questions. "But you'd better leave that knapsack here, little lady. Can't let you smuggle in a file, can we?"

No one was in the two-room cell block but Sogoji. I almost didn't recognize him, because he was wearing a suit and a bowler hat. The hat looked familiar—then I remembered the picture of his father propped up in the family shrine. That's probably where I'd seen the suit, too. The jacket and trousers were too big, but the hat fit just fine. It made him look a little like his father.

His smile breaking out made me want to cry again. "Hazel! You came!"

Not far enough. But I tried to smile back as I sat beside him on the narrow bunk against the wall. He sneezed—reminding me that I was probably responsible for that. "I'm sorry I told you to jump in the creek. I didn't think you'd have to really *do* it."

He wiped his nose, sniffling. "I was so scared. Could only think, what would Hazel do?"

I winced; that didn't sound like such a good rule to live by. "Are you still scared?"

He nodded over and over, and this time I gave in to the impulse I'd often felt—to reach out and put a hand at the back of his head and stop him. I didn't take the hand away but let it slide to his shoulder. Shyly he raised a hand to place on my shoulder, too. "I wanted to come with you," I said, "but they won't let me."

"It's not right that you go to jail."

My hand fell off his shoulder. "I'll tell you what's not right. It's not right for the U.S. government, or anybody else, to lock people up because of the way they look or what their last name is. It's not right to decide what you are because of your face. It's not right for anybody to keep friends apart."

"Not right to drop bombs on Pearl Harbor, either. Or make Jed missing in action."

"But you didn't have anything to do with any of that!"

He shrugged. "War will be over soon, let's hope."

"And then what happens to you?"

"A man came to talk to me last night. He says I am ward of the state. When I ask what's that, he says it's somebody under the care of U.S. government."

"Do you think—" I was almost afraid to say my greatest fear out loud. "Do you think they'll send you to Japan?"

He shook his head. "Nope. But I may have to live in installation."

"In what? Oh—you mean an institution? Like an orphanage?"

"*Hai.*" A look of doubt crossed his face. "Is that bad?"

A good thing he'd never read *Oliver Twist.* I tried to think of something to say that wouldn't scare him worse. "Can't you stay with a family here in Hood River?"

"Japanese family, maybe. The man says if some Japanese come back here and want to take me in, maybe I can be ward of them."

"That's what we'll do then." I felt a little quiver of hope. "While you're away, I'll find somebody."

"But, Hazel. Nobody wants Japanese to come back here."

"Not everybody feels that way." I stuck my hand in my pocket, feeling for the newspaper piece I'd put there, and my fingers closed around Jed's silver dollar as well. I pulled them both out and waved the paper at him. "Look at this. It's a letter to the editor. The writer says if the Japanese want to be good Americans, we should welcome them back." While he stared at the paper, I opened my hand to reveal the silver dollar. "At least you can take this."

As soon as he recognized it, he began shaking his head. "No, it's yours. You keep."

"*Look.*" There was something I had to make him understand—even though it wasn't too clear to me yet. "See the lady on the coin, with the sun rising behind her? That's Liberty. Freedom. And see what it says here: 'In God we trust.' You need to remember that. You're a prisoner now, like Jed is, maybe. But we need to trust that it'll all work out in time. And when you come back, you can give this silver dollar to me, and when Jed comes back, I'll return it to him. Then its work will be over."

He stared at the silver dollar, his face kind of screwed up with his thoughts. "That note I left for you in the tower. Did you see it?"

I nodded.

"Do you remember what I wrote on it?"

"Uh-huh. The flower fades, the mountain is forever. What's the mountain—Fuji-san?"

"No. Maybe no mountain at all. Stars, maybe? Heaven."

"Love?" I was speaking louder and faster. "Friendship?"

His face smoothed out. "God. Peace."

"*What* peace?"

"In the sky. Remember? We watched for it, you and me."

I remembered sitting on the tower beside a coal fire with him, and it seemed that peace was what we were watching for after all, in the very middle of the night.

I took his hand and dropped the silver dollar into it. "Yeah. We did." That clear, still beauty was in me yet. "Promise me you'll keep watching."

"I promise. Though many flowers fade."

* * *

After a while, two military policemen arrived to drive Sogoji to the railroad depot. I was hoping he could go quietly but somehow word got out. A handful of people had gathered on the station platform by the time Mr. Lanski and I walked over. With a start, I recognized Mr. Erickson was among them, and Owen. A boy ran past me—Sherman, coming from the direction of the newspaper office. Owen nudged him and nodded in my direction. They both looked surprised. My heart was pumping furiously as I stepped under the eaves of the station and stood next to the dispatcher's window. A chilly rain had started; I was shivering and sweating at the same time.

Mr. Lanski tapped on the window of the military sedan until one of the MPs rolled down the window partway. I heard him explaining that Sogoji was just an orphan kid who had no relatives and almost no experience of the world. Meaning, Don't let anything happen to him, please. The MP just nodded, snapping his gum and looking bored. When the train pulled in, they waited until the last minute to get Sogoji on it, in case an "incident" broke out at the sight of him. Even so, when the two MPs took him out of the backseat of the car and hustled him through the little crowd on the platform, I heard some angry words and saw some ugly looks. Maybe Sogoji shouldn't have worn those grown-up clothes after all; he might have earned more sympathy dressed in his usual scarecrow outfit.

When they paused for one of the MPs to give their military pass to the conductor, somebody tossed a rock that knocked the bowler hat to one side. A voice—Sherman's, I think—called out, "Go back where you came from, Jap!"

That did it. From now on my name at school would be Mud, but I broke away from Mr. Lanski's restraining arm and pushed through the crowd. When I reached Sogoji, I threw my arms around him. Even the MPs were taken by surprise.

"*Come* back where you came from," I whispered in his ear. "You belong where your friends are."

Just before they pulled me away, not too roughly, I felt his birdlike touch on the back of my head. When they bundled him into the train, he was blushing. But smiling, too.

I waved until the train pulled away, and Mr. Lanski walked up. "You don't exactly know how to lay low, do you?" he asked dryly.

"I had to do it." I glanced toward the corner of the platform, where Sherman was staring at me with a shocked expression. Owen looked smug (knowing all along I was a Jap lover), and Mr. Erickson scowled. A couple of little kids were giggling and an elderly lady shook her head. "And I'm not sorry," I added.

"Guess I'm not either." After a pause, Mr. Lanski put his hand on my shoulder, giving it a little squeeze. It was funny: the world was a lot bigger than me, like he said, but for the first time I knew I had a place in it. And I knew, without asking, that we could find a place for Sogoji, too. "Now let's go home," he said.

AUTHOR'S NOTE

Beginning in December 1944, reports of flaming objects in the sky over the northwestern United States began filtering in to army intelligence. Military investigators already knew something was up, since Coast Guard vessels in the Pacific had been scooping up fuses, bomb parts, and balloon scraps with Japanese markings. But what, exactly, were these scraps all about? When a bomb exploded over Thermopolis, Wyoming, on December 6, part of the mystery was solved: the enemy had finally targeted the mainland, as Americans long suspected they would.

But how? The Japanese had no long-range bombers that could cross the ocean. When two lumberjacks in Montana found a 33-foot-wide Japanese balloon in the forest, and another bomb exploded in southern Oregon leaving telltale debris, intelligence directors had their answer, unbelievable as it seemed. The Japanese were using balloons to float incendiary bombs! Even then, no one suspected they were coming all the way from Japan—it was assumed that they were being launched from submarines or uncharted Pacific islands, or perhaps even from within the United States. Not until the war was over did all the facts about the "Fu-go project" come to light: using the principles of seasonal wind currents and atmospheric pressure, Japanese scientists had figured out how to keep the balloons airborne all the way across the Pacific until some could reach the West Coast and drop their deadly payload.

The scheme was too iffy to expect widespread destruction on the American mainland. At best, the Japanese military hoped to start some forest fires and spread general panic. To prevent this, American military intelligence launched a secrecy campaign, alerting news services, radio stations, schools, and community groups to the danger but warning them to keep quiet. No newspaper or radio broadcast broke the story, and the Japanese never knew that their plan had actually succeeded until the war was over.

Unfortunately, not every American got the message. In May 1945, a family picnic near Bly, Oregon, ended in disaster when a Fu-go bomb exploded, killing a mother and five children. They were the only mainland casualties of the entire war. Soon after, the U.S. government went public with information about the balloon bombs. By then it didn't matter: the last one had been launched from Japan in April.

Another secret in the Northwest was being well kept during that time: the project to develop the world's first atomic bomb. At Hanford Engineering Works in Washington state, a nuclear reactor was turning out uranium slugs to be used in making plutonium. On March 10, 1945, the reactor accidentally shut down for one-fifth of a second. A longer delay would have caused a meltdown and possibly an explosion, terminating the project or setting it back for months. Searching for the cause of the shutdown, technicians found a piece of Japanese balloon tangled in the electrical line that powered the reactor. Six months later, almost to the day, the first atomic bomb was dropped on Hiroshima, Japan.

Unlike their parents, second-generation Japanese who were born in the United States (the *nisei*) were American citizens. However, their parents could apply to the Japanese government for dual citizenship at birth. That's one of the things that would need to be cleared up about Sogoji's status before he could return to Hood River. Once he did, his chances of being adopted into a returning Japanese family would have been very good. Many of those families who chose to return to Hood River (and many went elsewhere, even to Japan) found that their farms had been neglected by neighbors who had promised to take care of them. There was plenty of work to do. An extra pair of hands, especially energetic ones like Sogoji's, would have been welcome.

That doesn't mean it would have been easy for Sogoji. Even though the U.S. Justice Department had concluded, long before the war ended, that there was no evidence of subterfuge against the United States by the Japanese Americans, suspicions remained. Fair-minded people like the Reverend Sherman Burgoyne, Arline Moore, and the League for Liberty and Justice went out of their way to welcome back the exiles. But plenty of bad feelings remained to be overcome, and the returning Japanese Americans had to put up with snubs and slurs and store owners who refused to do business with them. Those scars have faded over the years, and some third-generation *sansei* still make their homes where their grandparents originally settled.

I'm indebted to Linda Tamura, a *sansei* herself, whose book (*The Hood River Issei*) and valuable comments helped me get a handle on the Japanese American experience. Also, many thanks to Connie Nice of the Hood River Historical Museum; Dave Burkhardt, retired from the agricultural extension; and my fellow children's author and Hood River native Pat Krusso. They corrected my assumptions about the area, though any inaccuracies that remain are mine alone. And thanks as always to Nancy, my most excellent editor, and her ever-ready assistant, Michele.